Creature Teacher

Look for more books in the Goosebumps Series 2000
by R.L. Stine:

Creature Teacher

R.L. Stine

Scholastic Children's Books
Commonwealth House, 1–19 New Oxford Street, London WC1A 1NU, UK
a division of Scholastic Ltd
London ~ New York ~ Toronto ~ Sydney ~ Auckland

First published in the USA by Scholastic Inc., 1998
First published in the UK by Scholastic Ltd, 1998

Copyright © Parachute Press, Inc., 1998
Goosebumps is a trademark of Parachute Press, Inc.

ISBN 0 590 11330 5

Typeset by Rowland Phototypesetting Ltd, Bury St Edmunds, Suffolk
Printed by Mackays of Chatham plc, Chatham, Kent

10 9 8 7 6 5 4 3 2 1

Prologue

You think you're safe in bed.

Outside your bedroom window, the wind moans, rattling the glass. You hear shrill animal howls. The steady tap of a tree branch against the wall of the house.

You don't care. Your bed is warm and soft. You pull the blankets higher. You settle your head into the pillow.

The wind and howls are outside, so far away.

You are safe and warm and cosy.

You don't see the slender green tendrils reaching up from under your bed. Glistening wetly in the moonlight from the window, they reach up ... stretch ... stretch ... like plant vines.

Your eyes are shut. You have a smile on your face.

You're thinking about something funny you said that made your mum and dad laugh out loud.

You don't see the long tendrils wrapping themselves over you. Coiling over your blankets like thick snakes.

You don't hear the grunts of the creature under your bed. You think it's the wind outside. You don't hear the creature grunting as it tightens its long tendrils around you.

The blankets are so thick, you don't feel the tendrils over you—until it's too late.

Now you can't move.

The creature grunts as it squeezes you. Its long green arms wrap you tighter . . . tighter.

You feel yourself sinking, sinking into a deep, deep darkness.

You open your mouth to scream. But no sound comes out.

The wet green tendrils slide tighter around you. Beneath the bed, the creature grunts and coughs.

You gasp for breath. Finally, you let out a scream. You open your mouth and scream and scream and scream.

When I was three and four, I had a lot of night-mares like that. Night after night, Mum and Dad would come running into my room. They would click on all the lights. Sit on my bed. Hold my hand and tell me it was only a dream.

"Monsters don't exist, Paul."

That's what they always said.

2

I suppose I believed in monsters when I was little. When you're four years old, you still have a lot to learn. You don't have a clue about what's real and what's fantasy.

I was afraid a lot of the time. I believed in ghosts, and monsters, and strange creatures.

The kid next door told me there was a mummy buried under my garage, and I believed him. I never went into the garage after dark.

I wouldn't swim in the lake on our family holiday. Mum and Dad couldn't *drag* me in. I imagined all the clammy, dark creatures waiting at the bottom, with claws and stingers and snapping jaws.

Okay, okay. Go ahead. Call me names. Paul Perez is a scaredy-cat. Paul Perez is a wimp.

I admit it. I suppose that's why I became a joker. I made jokes to help me get over my fears.

And I *did* get over my fears.

I learnt what's real and what's made up. I learnt to tell when the kid next door was teasing me.

I'm twelve now, and I don't have nightmares any more. I don't have to look under the bed before I go to sleep. The howling wind doesn't make me think I hear ghosts outside my window. And I can go into the garage any time of night or day.

I'm starting a new school tomorrow. I'm

leaving home for the first time to go to a boarding-school.

And I'm calm and cool about it. Sure, I'm excited. But I'm not afraid.

I know that most people are normal and nice wherever you go.

The world is normal and ordinary.

There is no such thing as monsters.

Monsters are for three-year-olds. Monsters are for babies.

Right?

Right?

"It wasn't my fault."

"No more excuses, Paul," Mum warned me.

"But I'm telling you, it wasn't my fault. It was Harold's fault."

Mum and Dad glanced at each other. They both shook their heads in disgust.

Okay. Maybe it *was* my fault.

I was the one who brought Harold, my talking parrot, to school.

And I was the one who taught him to say, *Don't do your work. The teacher's a jerk.*

But how was I supposed to know he'd say it in the middle of class? And say it and say it and say it?

I told Miss Hammett I was sorry. I told her Harold made it up on his own.

Did she believe that?

No way.

She dragged me to the head-teacher's office. And guess what Cool Paul did on the way there?

I tripped her.

She fell over my foot and cracked her knee on the tiled floor. She howled in pain until two other teachers helped her up and carried her away.

It was an accident, I swear. I'm really clumsy. I told Miss Hammett that I didn't do it on purpose. She didn't believe me.

She tortured me after that. She gave me extra homework. She always called on me first and embarrassed me every chance she had.

I tried to change her mind about me. I tried to make her laugh. That's what I always do to win people over.

"Mr Perez, please spell 'Mississippi' for the class."

"The river or the state?"

That's a pretty funny joke . . . isn't it?

She glared at me angrily, as if I had burped or something.

I tried again. I tried lots of times. The kids laughed. But Miss Hammett never cracked a smile.

"Miss Hammett is nuts. She hates me. I'll never get good grades with her," I complained to my parents.

Mum and Dad care a lot about good grades. They are both super-achievers.

Dad was made president of his company last

year. Mum is a lawyer, but she doesn't practise. She writes long, serious articles about the law in all the big law journals. And she goes on TV shows to talk about all the major courtroom trials.

Get the picture?

My parents are serious people. I know they stare at me and wonder how they got such a joker for a son. I know they are disappointed in me.

As soon as they heard I was having trouble at school, they went and talked with Miss Hammett and the head. The next week, they announced they wanted to give me a better opportunity.

"We've picked out an excellent boarding-school for you," Dad said.

"The school normally takes only the best students in the country," Mum added. "But your dad made some phone calls and pulled a few strings. They're going to take you on a trial basis."

"I'm on trial?" I cried. "Do I get my own lawyer?"

See. I always joke when I'm nervous.

"Maybe I could just apologize to Miss Hammett again," I suggested. "Maybe I could get Harold to apologize too."

"Miss Hammett isn't the problem," Dad said. "The problem is your attitude, Paul. You need a school where you can be serious and discover your true interests and talents."

"You need to prove to yourself that you can achieve your goals," Mum added.

I told you. We're talking *serious* with a capital "S"!

My heart was pounding. I suddenly felt cold all over. I didn't want to leave home. I didn't want to be in a strange school with a whole class of serious, straight-A students!

"What's the school called?" I asked.

"The Caring Academy," Dad replied. He held up a brochure with a photo on the front. I glimpsed a big stone building on top of a hill. It looked like Dracula's castle or something.

"The *Caring* Academy?" I cried shrilly. "What kind of sick name is that? It sounds like a hospital!"

"It was founded by the Caring family," Mum replied. "They are an old New England family. They started the school in 1730."

"That's too old," I grumbled. "I bet the toilets don't work."

That was supposed to be funny. But they didn't laugh.

"This is a great second chance for you, Paul," Dad said, putting a hand on my shoulder. "It was really hard to convince them to take you. I know you'll try your best."

"But—why boarding-school?" I stammered.

8

"I've never gone away to school. I've never even gone to camp!"

Dad kept his arm on my shoulder. He walked me towards the living-room. "It's a tough world out there, Paul," he said softly, as if telling me a secret.

He frowned. "The world gets tougher and tougher. It's eat or be eaten."

I stared at him, trying to figure out what he was telling me.

Eat or be eaten.

Eat or be eaten.

I didn't really understand him.

I had no way of knowing just how soon those words would come *true*!

"'The Caring Academy'." I read the name on the tall iron gate as we drove through. "I wonder what the football team is called. Probably the Caring Goody-Goodies. Or the Caring Cuties!"

I know that was lame. But I laughed at my own joke. I was so nervous, I was bouncing in the back seat like a baby! I couldn't sit still.

"This is a serious academic school," Mum said. "There is no football team, Paul."

The school really did look like Dracula's castle. It even had two tall, grey stone towers on each end. "If you're bad, we'll lock you in the tower!" I cried in my scary-movie voice.

My parents ignored me.

The sky stretched heavy and grey. A few large raindrops spattered the windscreen of our van. The narrow road led us into a dark court-yard. Lightning crackled over the dark tower. It really reminded me of an old horror movie.

"Why did they build the school up here on

this hill?" I demanded. "It's miles from the nearest town."

"Maybe they liked the view," Dad replied. His idea of a joke.

"They probably wanted privacy," Mum said.

A few minutes later, we were inside the old school. To my surprise, it was bright and cheery. The walls were a warm yellow, covered with colourful posters. Each door down the long hallway had been painted a different colour.

A big, broad-shouldered man with bushy grey hair and thick, black-framed glasses hurried through the crowded hallway to introduce himself. "I'm Mr Klane, the Dean of Students," he boomed. "Let me help you with those bags."

Under his woolly white sweater, he had bulging biceps and an enormous chest. He looked like a middle-aged Clark Kent. He picked up my heavy trunk in one hand and led us to my room.

"The dormitories are in this wing," he explained. "The classrooms are at the other end." His deep voice echoed through the long hall. He leant close to me. "The torture chamber is downstairs," he whispered.

I stared at him.

He threw back his head and laughed. "Be careful, Paul," he warned. "Your fellow students are all so smart and sharp. And they *love* playing tricks on the new kid."

As we made our way down the hall, I checked out the kids. They all appeared perfectly normal. A lot of baggy jeans and khakis, T-shirts, sweaters, unbuttoned waistcoats. Tommy Hilfiger and The Gap. No different from the kids in my old school.

What did you expect, Paul? I asked myself. Everyone walking around in Beethoven shirts, reading from encyclopaedias as they walked through the halls?

We turned into another long hall. Mum and Dad followed behind Mr Klane and me, carrying my stuff. We passed an office door marked CARING ACADEMY HEADMISTRESS. "You'll meet her later," Mr Klane said.

Students scurried out of his way. He carried my huge trunk as if it were a lunch box!

As we approached, a short, squat, weird-looking kid backed into a doorway. He had a round, pale face, tiny black eyes and straight, slicked-down black hair parted in the middle. He reminded me of a mole, one of those lumpy pink animals that lives underground.

"What are you doing here, Marv?" Mr Klane snapped at him. Before the boy could answer, Mr Klane gave him a push. "Get going now. You know you don't belong over here."

The boy mumbled something under his breath. He slumped away. He had a funny, shuffling walk. He looked like a bowling ball on legs.

Mr Klane watched the boy until he vanished around a corner. Then he began walking again, taking long strides. "What is your special interest, Paul?"

"Huh? Special what?" I hurried to keep up with him.

"Special study interest," he said. "What area of study—?"

"Lunch?" I joked.

I glimpsed Mum and Dad scowling and shaking their heads unhappily. "Paul hasn't really discovered his *passion*," Mum told Mr Klane.

My passion? Yuck. I wanted to throw up.

Mr Klane nodded. "We have a very talented student body here, Paul," he said. "Wonderful kids. Wonderful. My only complaint about them is that they study *too hard*!"

Oh, great, I thought sarcastically. Just my kind of place.

Am I doomed or am I doomed?

"Here is your room," Mr Klane announced, pushing open a blue door. We stepped into a small, bright room with two beds, two dressing-tables, two desks and a small red-leather sofa.

"You'll be sharing the room with a nice boy called Brad Caperton," Mr Klane announced. He dropped the trunk on to the bed against the far wall. "Brad is practising his violin now. He'll be up when he's finished."

"A lovely room," Mum commented, walking

around. "And you have a room-mate, Paul. Isn't that lucky?"

"Do you play an instrument?" Mr Klane asked me.

I shook my head. "I tried playing a harmonica once, but I swallowed it!"

Mr Klane laughed. My first laugh of the day. Unfortunately, this time I wasn't joking!

Outside the narrow window, lightning flickered. A boom of thunder shook the room.

Mum and Dad started to unpack my things. Mr Klane studied me through his thick, black-framed glasses. "It's hard starting a new school in November," he said. "But you'll catch up. Work hard, and you'll catch up."

"Paul plans to work very hard," Dad said, eyeing me sternly.

"I have to get to the front office now," Mr Klane said, checking his watch. He shook hands with Mum and Dad. "A pleasure to meet you."

He turned back to me at the doorway. "I'll send a couple of classmates to show you to your classroom. Good luck, Paul." He vanished out of the door.

Thunder shook the room again. The lights flickered but didn't go out.

The next half hour flew by. We unpacked my stuff. We hugged. We said goodbye. We hugged again.

And then Mum and Dad were gone. And I was left in this dark castle on top of a hill. Trapped in a school of overachieving violin players who studied too hard!

I suddenly thought about Harold. My poor parrot, all alone at home with no one to teach him new funny things to say.

"Don't do your work. Teacher's a jerk!" I did my best Harold imitation. I sounded just like him.

I heard giggling. Spun round. And saw two girls in the doorway.

"I . . . was doing a parrot," I explained. I could feel my face turning red hot. I knew I was blushing.

"I'm Celeste Majors," one of them said. She was short with piles of curly blonde hair and lots of freckles. Her green eyes sparkled behind round, wire-rimmed glasses.

Celeste was a purple person. Purple turtleneck sweater, purple jeans and purple Doc Martens.

The other girl introduced herself as Molly Bagby. She was tall and very thin, with long, straight black hair and a black fringe that fell down over her eyes.

Molly wore jeans too—black, with a hole in each knee—and a red sweatshirt under a black leather waistcoat. Three small silver hoop earrings dangled from one ear.

"Mr Klane asked us to show you to the class-room," Molly said. "Are you ready?"

I nodded. "I suppose so."

I started for the door.

But to my surprise, the girls hurried into the room and slammed the door behind them.

Celeste glanced tensely behind her. She turned to Molly. "Did anyone see us?"

"I—I don't think so," Molly replied. "Listen—Paul?" Her eyes locked on mine. "You've got to hurry," she said in a whisper.

"Huh? Hurry?" I gaped at the two of them.

Why did they look so frightened?

"Listen to us," Celeste whispered, glancing back at the door. "Get out of here!"

"What—?" I started.

"Don't ask questions," Molly insisted through clenched teeth. Her chin trembled. "Just get *away* from this school, Paul. Get away while you still can!"

Celeste grabbed my arm. She shoved me towards the door. "Maybe your parents haven't left. Maybe you can still catch them!"

"But—but—" I sputtered.

"Hurry!" Molly cried.

I pulled open the door—and bumped into Mr Klane. I staggered back. I felt as if I'd collided with a truck.

"You're still in here," he said, gazing from Molly to Celeste. "Is there a problem?"

"No. No problem," Celeste replied quickly, tugging down the sleeves of her purple sweater. "We were just telling Paul—"

"We were telling him where everything is," Molly cut in. "You know. The gym. The canteen."

"Good." Mr Klane smiled at me. "But you don't want Paul to be late for his class. Mrs Maaargh wouldn't like that."

Mrs *Who*? I wondered.

Mr Klane held the door open. The girls led

the way down the hall. He followed us the whole way, whistling a tune to himself.

The girls didn't say a word.

We walked past the front entrance and then into the brightly coloured classroom wing. Kids with rucksacks were hurrying into rooms.

I suddenly started to laugh. I'd finally realized what Molly and Celeste were doing. They were playing a little "welcome" joke on the new kid.

Mr Klane had warned me to watch out. He'd said the old-timers like to play tricks on newcomers.

Wow, they really fooled me! I thought. They really had me scared for a moment.

I could see them both staring at me as we walked. They were wondering why I was laughing. I didn't say a word. I'm not as stupid as I look, I decided.

We stepped into a classroom. Room 333. At first, I thought we were late. I thought class had already begun, because it was so silent in the room.

But I couldn't see a teacher at the front of the room.

I saw several kids with their heads buried in books, reading intently. Two kids leant over their desks, typing furiously on laptops. A few others were scribbling in notebooks.

I followed Molly and Celeste into the room.

"Mrs Maaargh will be here any second," Celeste whispered, pushing back her blonde curls. "Whatever you do, don't get her angry."

"Be careful—" Molly started to warn.

She was interrupted by a tall, good-looking boy with spiky brown hair. He stepped up behind her and bumped into her playfully from behind. "Stop it, Brad," she snapped.

"Hey, how's it going?" Brad asked me. "I'm your room-mate. Did you find the room and everything?"

"Yeah. No problem," I replied. "But there wasn't enough space for all my stuff, so I dumped some of yours out in the hall."

Brad stared at me for a moment. When he realized I was joking, he laughed. Molly and Celeste didn't join in. They kept glancing tensely at the classroom door.

"We'd better sit down," Molly whispered. "Mrs Maaargh likes to find us in our seats."

I turned—and gasped when I saw a pair of legs dangling from the ceiling. Gazing up, I saw a boy—hanging—hanging by a rope.

No.

Not a boy.

A dummy. Just a dummy. I glanced round quickly, hoping that Brad and the girls hadn't heard my gasp. I felt so embarrassed that I'd been fooled.

The dummy had a sign attached to its waist.

It read: HANG AROUND FOR THE TALENT SHOW, FRIDAY, NOVEMBER 18.

Brad saw me staring at it. "What's your talent, Paul?" he asked.

"Talent? Uh . . . I don't really have one," I confessed.

All three of them stared at me. "No talent?" Molly cried, pushing back her black fringe. "You can't be admitted to Caring without a talent."

I didn't know what to say. I didn't want to tell them that my dad had called a few people to get me in. "What's your talent?" I asked Molly, to make them stop staring at me.

Molly frowned. "Well, I have a little problem. I play the violin. And so does Brad."

"That's a problem?" I asked.

She nodded solemnly. "Mrs Maaargh says only one violinist per show. Brad and I have to audition. The winner gets to be in the show. The loser has to find another talent."

"Don't worry about it," Brad assured Molly. "You're so much better than me. You'll win easily."

Molly let out a little cry. "I wish we both could win, Brad. I—I'm so *frightened*."

"Hey, it's just a show," I cut in. "Right?"

No one answered me. All round us, kids sat with their faces pressed into their books.

"I'm a singer," Celeste told me. "So far,

there's just one singer. So I'm safe. You're not a singer, are you, Paul?"

"No way," I said. "My dad says I can't carry a tune in a bucket. Why is everyone so worried about the talent show?"

Again, no one answered. All three of them turned to the door. Still no sign of the teacher.

"You've got to find a talent," Brad said. "If you don't. . ." His voice trailed off.

They're trying to scare me, I realized. They're having some fun. Trying to scare the new kid.

"I've *got* a talent!" I exclaimed. "I'm a dancer. I'm an awesome dancer!"

I reached up with both hands, tugged the dummy off its rope, and started to dance with it. I threw its arms round my neck, clutched its waist, and began to twirl in a circle, humming loudly.

I expected the class to burst out laughing. I expected some cheers, some applause.

Back at my old school, the kids would have gone berserk!

But here, most of the kids didn't even glance up. They kept reading their books and scribbling their notes.

I pressed the dummy's face against mine and strutted it across the room in a crazy tango.

No laughs. No cheers. Brad, Molly and Celeste gaped at me, eyes wide, faces frozen in horror.

21

What is their problem? I wondered. This is *funny*!

I did a wild spin. "OOOPS!" The dummy slid from my hands.

I grabbed for it. Tripped over it. And stumbled to the floor on top of it.

The room remained completely silent.

I raised my head. Started to roll off the dummy.

But I stopped when I saw a massive figure filling the doorway.

Mrs Maaargh!

On top of the dummy on my hands and knees on the floor, I stared up at her. She wore a shiny red dress. She was so wide, she blocked all the light from the hall.

She narrowed watery brown eyes at me. And growled, "You must be Paul."

I could see everyone staring at me now. Even the kids who'd been pounding away on laptops had raised their heads to watch me.

I picked myself up from the floor. "Sorry," I muttered. I bent to pick up the dummy. But Mrs Maaargh motioned with a big hand for me to leave it on the floor.

"Come here, Paul." She had a gravelly voice. It sounded like she had marbles rolling around in her throat.

I hesitated, squinting at the bright red dress that filled the doorway.

"Come here, Paul," she repeated. The watery brown eyes stayed on me. She didn't blink. Her lumpy, round face had no expression at all. "Come here."

I glimpsed Molly and Celeste. Their features were set, jaws clenched, eyes wide—with fright?

I shoved my hands into my jeans pockets and made my way slowly to the doorway. "I was just kidding around with the dummy," I explained.

Mrs Maaargh nodded. "Let me have a taste," she said softly.

I swallowed hard. *What* did she say?

"Come here, Paul," she repeated. "Let me have a taste."

I heard Celeste utter a soft cry behind me.

I didn't hear another sound. The room grew so silent, I could hear the soft scrape of my trainers on the wooden floor as I crossed the room.

I stepped up to Mrs Maaargh. I flashed her my best smile. "Hi," I said.

She grabbed my arm. Pulled my hand from my pocket.

Then, with a low grunt, she lowered her head. Stuck out a fat pink tongue, glistening wet and as wide as a cow's tongue.

And she licked my arm all the way from the wrist to my shoulder.

23

I heard sick groans from the kids behind me. But when I turned back, they all had their heads down, pretending not to be watching.

Yuck.

My arm tingled. It felt sticky and wet.

Mrs Maaargh let go of me. She grinned. Thick gobs of saliva clung to her teeth.

"Tasty." I *think* that's what she said.

My mouth dropped open in shock. I couldn't believe it. Had she just *licked* me?

I just stood there, staring at her.

She was so weird looking! She had the biggest head I've ever seen on a human. She had thick brown hair piled on top of it, with a pencil stuck through the top.

She stared back at me with wet brown eyes. Cow's eyes. She had pale yellow skin, like the skin on chickens in the supermarket. Her cheeks were so flabby, they bounced on her neck as she grinned. Her whole face sagged over her shoulders like dough.

"You may take a seat, Paul," she said finally, in that rattly voice. She pointed. "Take that seat near the back."

I was so glad to get away from her! I turned and walked as fast as I could towards the back. "Did you see that? She *licked* me!" I whispered to Celeste as I passed by her seat.

She stared straight ahead and pretended not to hear me. Her hands were gripping the desk-top so tightly, her knuckles were white.

It's *Play a Joke on the New Kid*, I told myself.

In a short while, we'll all have a big laugh over this.

But none of the kids were even smiling.

As I stepped into the back row, I noticed a line of wire cages on a table against the wall. Inside the cages, I saw a white bunny, some kind of tiny grey squirrel, a guinea pig and a white mouse.

Aren't we a little *old* for classroom animals? I asked myself.

I carefully stepped over a red-haired girl's feet and squeezed in front of a solemn-looking boy who didn't look up from his textbook.

I slid into the empty seat, dropping my ruck-sack beside me. The wooden desk was scratched and cracked. In one corner, someone had carved two words deep into the wood: HELP ME.

I rubbed my finger over the words. And glanced to the front of the room.

To my surprise, Mrs Maaargh was still in the doorway. She hadn't moved. Is she too big to get through the door? I wondered.

"We'll start with our grammar homework today," she announced. "Paul, I'm sure someone in the class will be happy to help you catch up."

With a grunt, she squeezed her body through the doorway. The red dress bounced up and down as she moved. Stand-up comics on TV always joke about a woman's dress being as big as a tent. But this dress really did look like a shiny red tent.

Her chins bobbed. Her tall hair bounced and shook.

And as Mrs Maaargh walked to her desk, I heard a wet, smacking sound. *SMACK*. *SMACK*.

Leaning across my desk, I lowered my eyes to the sound—and gasped.

Mrs Maaargh was barefoot!

Her feet were *huge*! As big and puffy as pillows!

They made disgusting, wet smacking noises against the wooden floor.

"Ohhhhh." I let out a low moan, watching those weird, bare feet. No toes! No toes!

Instead, thick, shiny black claws curled out from the tops.

I felt sick. A wave of nausea rolled up from my stomach.

And then the teacher's rattly growl broke through the silence: "What are you looking at, Paul? You got a *problem*?"

My heart beat hard against my chest. I turned my eyes to Celeste, then to Molly. Had they seen those disgusting feet?

They sat very straight, eyes locked on Mrs Maaargh's face.

I searched for Brad and found him in the front row. He was tapping a pencil on his desk, very casual, pretending everything was okay.

I turned back to Mrs Maaargh. I tried not to stare down at her feet. But I did. I couldn't help it.

"Well, what are you staring at?" Mrs Maaargh demanded again.

"Huh—me?" I could feel beads of sweat form on my forehead. "I'm staring at . . . nothing." My voice came out in a choked whisper.

Mrs Maaargh shook her blobby head from side to side. "Didn't anyone tell you I'm a monster?"

My heart raced now. "Well. . ."

Mrs Maaargh marched to the chart at the front of the room. Her feet smacked the floor wetly with each lumbering step.

She picked up a long pointer and jabbed it at the top of the chart, at the big black words: FOOD CHAIN.

"Can anyone explain to Paul abut the food chain?" she growled. Her big cow's eyes moved across the room. "Mary?"

Mary was the red-haired girl at the end of my row. "The big eat the little," she said timidly. "I mean, the powerful eat the less powerful."

Mrs Maaargh tapped the chart impatiently with the long pointer. "That's not quite the way I'd describe it," she said gruffly. "I'd say that the higher species eat the lower species."

Brad raised his hand. "Little fish eat plankton," he said. "And bigger fish eat the little fish. And even *bigger* fish eat the big fish."

"And *people* eat the biggest fish!" a chubby boy near the window declared.

"And monsters eat people!" Mrs Maaargh roared. Her doughy face bobbed up and down as she opened her mouth in a long, loud laugh.

No one else in the room joined in.

I squinted at the chart. I saw twenty or twenty-five rectangular white cards down from the top. A name on each card. The names of everyone in the class.

Is it some kind of achievement chart? I

wondered. We had one of those in second grade. Everyone got gold or silver stars.

Kind of babyish for sixth grade!

"Paul, do you know what a bottom feeder is?" Mrs Maaargh's raspy baritone interrupted my thoughts.

I gulped. "Well, in a lake or the ocean . . . it's a fish that swims along the bottom and eats things." I wiped sweat off my forehead with the back of my hand.

"Yes, that's right." Mrs Maaargh grinned. "It isn't good to be on the bottom—is it, class?"

Some kids shook their heads. Some muttered, "No."

"If you're on the bottom, you're going to be eaten!" Mrs Maaargh exclaimed excitedly.

I saw Molly grab her forehead, as if she had a bad headache. Beside her, Celeste covered her mouth with both hands.

"Paul, you've come to a school where the students like to be on top," Mrs Maaargh continued. As she talked, she tapped the food chain chart with the pointer. "And in my class, everyone works really hard to stay on top."

She leant forward, chins bobbing, wet eyes locked on me. "Because, guess what, Paul? I'm a bottom feeder! That's right! After the talent show in about three weeks—I'm going to check the food chain. I'm going to see who is at the very bottom. *And then I'm going to have a feast!*"

Her whole body shook as she roared with laughter. She howled and slapped her knees, which made her dress bounce around as if it were filled with footballs.

I laughed too. I mean, the whole idea was very funny.

It was a cruel joke to play on the new student. But it was a very funny joke. And I bet it scared a lot of new kids who didn't realize it was just a joke.

But I'm a joker, remember. And you can't kid a kidder. I knew what was going on.

"It's good!" I cried. "It's very funny! I'm shaking! Oooh, I'm shaking!"

Mrs Maaargh cut her laughter short. Her smile faded to an angry scowl. "What's funny?" she growled.

"The whole thing," I replied. "I mean, the chart and everything."

"Is there a joke here that I'm missing?" Mrs Maaargh asked, turning to the whole class. "Somebody, please tell me the joke. I like a good laugh. What's funny?"

Silence. The chubby kid next to me coughed. No one said a word.

"Were you laughing at *me*, Paul?" Mrs Maaargh demanded. "Does something about me strike you as *funny*?"

"No—!" I cried. "But the food chain—"

"Yes? The food chain?" She smacked the

pointer so hard against the chart, it split in two. Then she waved the broken pointer at me.

"Swim as hard as you can, Paul," she growled. "Swim as high as you can. Because after the talent show on the eighteenth, I'm going to see who is at the bottom of the food chain. And I'm going to *pig out* on whomever it is!"

"Good deal!" I cried, laughing. "I'll bring the barbecue sauce!"

No one laughed. What was *wrong* with these kids? That was funny!

The whole thing was funny.

Wasn't it?

Celeste had a finger to her lips. She began motioning frantically for me to shut up.

But I wasn't going to fall for this joke. No way.

"Can we roast marshmallows afterwards?" I asked.

Again, no laugh. No one even cracked a smile.

These kids were good actors!

Mrs Maaargh bent over her desk. I could see that she was writing something. After a few seconds, she held it up. A white card. Printed on it was my name: PAUL PEREZ.

"I put Velcro on the back of these so I can move them around," she told me. "I'm putting your name at the *top* of the food chain, Paul, since you're new."

With quick, sharp rips, Mrs Maaargh moved all the other cards down one space to make room for mine. I watched as she smacked my name on to the chart, pressing down on it to make sure it hung securely in place.

"That isn't fair!" a thin, pale girl near the door protested. "I worked hard to be on top. Why should he take my place?"

"Don't worry, Sharon," Mrs Maaargh replied. "I have a feeling he won't be up there for long."

"Put him on the bottom!" the chubby boy in my row shouted.

"Put him on the bottom! Put him on the bottom!" a few kids began to chant.

Wow, I thought. These people are taking the joke too far—aren't they? I mean, let it drop. It really isn't funny any more.

"Okay, students!" Mrs Maaargh clapped her hands together once. They made a wet, smacking sound like her bare feet. "Fun time is over. It's time to get down to work."

I shook my head. *Fun time?*

Scare the New Kid? That was fun time?

"As I said, we'll start today with the grammar homework," Mrs Maaargh announced.

She turned to the blackboard and wrote: WON'T YOU COME TO MY HOUSE? I WOULD LOVE TO HAVE YOU FOR LUNCH!

"Who would like to do this one?" she asked.

Every hand in the class shot up. I couldn't believe it! Some kids raised *both* hands!

"Pick me!"

33

"Please—pick me!"

Talk about teacher's pets!

"Paul, please approach the blackboard," Mrs Maaargh growled. "Let's see if you can tell the difference between subjects and verbs."

Why couldn't she pick on someone else? Every other kid in class *wanted* to go up there. Why pick on me?

I hesitated.

"Quickly now!" She slapped the blackboard with her meaty fist. It left a wet, round stain on the board.

I slowly stood and walked to the front of the classroom.

I could feel everyone's eyes on me. Celeste flashed me a thumbs-up as I passed her desk.

"If he messes up, call on me!" Brad called out.

Great room-mate!

"No—call on me!"

"No—me!"

What was their problem? I supposed these kids just *loved* competing!

"Here you go." Mrs Maaargh held out a piece of chalk.

I took another step—and heard a horrifying *SQUISH*.

My foot sank into something soft.

With a gasp, I stared down. And cried out, "Nooooo! Oh, no!"

"Owwwww!" Mrs Maaargh opened her mouth in a howl of pain.

I had stepped on her foot.

My trainer sank deep into the mushy flesh. I had to struggle to pull it out!

I staggered back, bumping into the blackboard.

She plopped into her chair and leant over to examine her foot. With a low moan, she ran her fingers over the wet skin.

"I'm—I'm sorry," I stammered. "I didn't mean to do that. I can't help it. I'm really clumsy."

Mrs Maaargh lifted her head and gazed at me with those watery brown cow's eyes. "You're off to a bad start," she groaned. "Remember what I said about swimming as high and as hard as you can?"

She stared down at her foot and rubbed it a bit more. Then she picked something up from the floor. "Owww. This will take *weeks* to grow back."

I let out a horrified moan when I saw what she was holding.

A broken piece of black, shiny claw.

She rolled it between her fingers, studying it.

I glanced at her foot. Four long claws curled on to the floor. The last claw, the claw I had stepped on, stuck up, a jagged stub now.

With a flick of her wrist, she threw the broken piece of claw into her mouth—and *ate* it.

I let out a gasp.

Mrs Maaargh stood up.

She limped past me, over to the food chain chart—and moved my name down two spots.

She hobbled back to her seat. But before she sat down, she reached out for my arm. And pinched it.

"Eat a big lunch, Paul," she rasped. "I want you to fatten up—okay?"

When the lunch bell rang, I couldn't wait to get out of there. But I saw a lot of kids make a bee-line for Mrs Maaargh.

"That was a great class today!" the red-haired girl gushed.

"This class is the best!" another girl declared.

Mrs Maaargh grinned. She seemed to be eating it all up.

Yuck! I thought. "Teacher's pet" isn't the

term for these kids. They are really disgusting! Are they all so desperate for A's that they have to act like total geeks?

"I think that new boy should start at the bottom," I heard a girl say.

"Yes. Put him on the bottom," another girl agreed.

I couldn't bear to hear any more. The joke had gone far enough. It wasn't funny any more. And I planned to tell that to Mrs Maaargh after lunch.

Where was the canteen? I hated first days in a new school! I couldn't find my *shadow* without someone helping me!

Luckily, I spotted Molly and Celeste. I hurried to catch up with them.

"Bad day, huh?" Celeste said, shaking her head.

"Not great," I agreed. "Mrs Maaargh is so weird! Don't you think—"

"What are *you* complaining about?" Molly wailed. "Did you see where I am on the food chain? Second from the bottom. If I mess up my violin audition on Sunday, I'm *toast*! I'll be that monster's dinner!"

"Cut! Cut!" I cried. "Can we take a break? The joke is getting really tired."

"Joke?" Molly tilted her head and squinted at me. Her black fringe tilted too. "What joke? Paul, if you think she's kidding—"

I didn't hear the rest. A group of boys across the hall burst out laughing and drowned out the rest of what Molly was saying.

By the time we reached the food queue in the canteen, it stretched for at least a mile. "Food must be good here," I joked. "Do they have Mystery Meat Surprise? That's my favourite!"

After we'd finally loaded up our trays, we couldn't find three seats together. So Molly and Celeste sat together. I told them it was okay. I'd find another spot.

I scanned the vast, noisy room and found an empty seat at the other end.

"Hi," I said to a pudgy boy with black, slicked-down hair, who sat opposite me. He was hunched over his lunch, shovelling it in with short, rapid movements, his round face nearly in the plate.

Why did he look familiar?

"Hey," he mumbled with a mouthful of spaghetti. He kept his eyes on his food.

I took a bite out of my egg salad sandwich. "My name is Paul," I told him.

"Marv," he muttered, finally peering up from his lunch. He had tiny, black eyes and a wide, crooked nose.

Marv, I thought to myself. That's the kid Mr Klane had shooed away when he led us to my room.

Marv and I ate quietly for a few minutes.

"I'm new here. Today is my first day." I tried to make conversation.

Marv squinted up at me. He had spaghetti sauce on his round cheeks. "You sure you want to sit here?" he asked.

"Yeah," I said. "Why not?"

He shrugged. "Who's your teacher?" He took a noisy slurp from his milk container.

"Mrs Maaargh," I told him. "And she's really weird." I lowered my voice. "She says she's a monster."

"Tell me about it." Marv rolled his eyes.

"Have you ever had her?" I asked.

"No way!" Marv picked up a meatball in his hand and threw it into his mouth. "I'm in Mr Thomerson's class," he said, swallowing it without chewing.

"You don't know how lucky you are!" I declared. "Mrs Maaargh doesn't wear shoes— and she has the grossest feet I've ever seen."

Marv nodded.

"Those feet are sickening," I went on. "They look like water balloons. And they have curly, black claws growing out of them."

I spotted Celeste and Molly across the room. Celeste was waving at me, waving me over.

Maybe a seat had opened up there. I started to get up.

Then I changed my mind. I wanted to stay and talk to Marv. Find out more about him.

Maybe find out if he knew anything about Mrs Maaargh.

"I don't know what's worse—her feet or her food chain chart," I continued.

"They're both bad," Marv said. "Really bad."

Celeste continued to wave at me from across the room. I nodded to her, to let her know I'd seen her. But I continued to talk to Marv.

"You know about the food chain chart?" I asked.

Marv nodded.

"It's some kind of joke, right?"

Marv shook his head no.

"Give me a break," I groaned. "She's not really going to eat someone after the talent show."

"Probably will," Marv said with a mouthful of spaghetti.

"Oh, sure." I rolled my eyes. "Did she eat someone here last year?"

"No," Marv said. "She didn't eat anyone here last year."

"Right," I replied quickly. "Because it's all a stupid joke."

"She didn't eat anyone here last year, because this is her *first year* at this school," Marv said.

"Oh."

Celeste began jumping up and down, waving frantically now. Molly started waving too.

What is their problem? I wondered.

Marv started telling me about his teacher. He said Mr Thomerson was a really nice man. I took another bite of my sandwich—and felt a tug from behind.

It was Celeste.

She grabbed my arm and dragged me across the room away from Marv's table.

"What are you doing, Paul?" she demanded. "Why are you sitting with Mrs Maaargh's son?"

Huh?

I'd been sitting with Mrs Maaargh's son?

And I'd told him that his mother was a monster?

Good move, Paul.

That will move you up *really* high on the food chain!

"What have I done?" I moaned.

I didn't really care about the food chain. I knew that was a stupid joke. But why was I at this boarding-school? Because I had got off to such a bad start with my teacher at the old school.

I couldn't get off to a bad start with this teacher. I couldn't. My parents would *kill* me!

"I told Mrs Maaargh's son that his mother was ugly and weird!" I cried.

"Don't worry," Celeste said softly. "I'm sure Marv won't say anything to his mother."

"What do you think?" I asked Molly.

"I think Celeste is a terrible liar."

"You mean—"

She brushed back her black fringe. "Marv is very close to his mother. He's probably telling her what you said right now!"

"What am I going to do?" I wailed.

Celeste bit her lip. She shook her head. "You're in big trouble. I tried to warn you."

Molly shrugged. "Maybe she'll only move you down a few notches. Don't worry. You won't slide down as far as me!" She sighed unhappily.

"I know! I'll go and see Mrs Maaargh right now!" I declared. "I'll apologize to her—before Marv has a chance to tell her what I said about her."

"Do you really think that's a good idea?" Celeste asked. "What if. . .?"

I didn't give her a chance to finish. I took off down the hall.

I had to get to the classroom fast. Before Marv had a chance to talk to his mother.

What would I say?

I'll think of something, I told myself. Mainly, I have to apologize.

I stopped outside the classroom door.

I took a few deep breaths for courage.

Then I stepped into the room. "Mrs Maaargh—?" I called.

I spotted her at the back of the room by the animal cages. She was bent over a cage, humming to herself.

"Mrs Maaargh?" I took a few steps closer.

She didn't seem to hear me. She was muttering in a low voice, muttering and humming.

I saw a lunch plate on top of the mouse cage. The plate had several square crackers set out on it. Beneath it, the mouse stared out, twitching its pointy nose.

I crept closer.

What was she doing?

I could hear her words now. "Here comes the bottom feeder," she sang into one of the cages. "Who's at the bottom now?"

And then, before I realized what was happening, she had the white mouse in her hand.

She raised it in both hands.

Opened her mouth wide.

And *bit off* the mouse's head!

It happened so fast—the mouse didn't utter a squeak.

And as I stared in amazement, Mrs Maaargh popped the tiny round mouse head from her mouth. She turned, carried it over to the plate, and placed it carefully on a cracker.

She lifted the cracker from the plate.

And saw me!

"Ohhhhh." I let out a moan and sank back.

"Paul!" Mrs Maaargh cried. She held up the cracker with the little white mouse head perched on it. "Paul—want an appetizer?"

She really is a monster!

In that moment, I knew the horrible truth. I didn't need to see any more to convince me.

But I *did* see more.

I saw her shove the cracker into her mouth, chew it up, enjoying it immensely, and swallow it.

My stomach lurched. I could taste egg salad at the back of my throat.

I clapped my hands over my mouth, whirled around—and ran.

I collided with Marv at the doorway. I nearly knocked him over.

"Hey—" he called out.

But I didn't stop. I took off down the hall, dodging and weaving through the groups of kids.

She really is a monster. I finally caught on to the truth.

She's a monster, and she really is going to eat one of us.

She's a monster, and she already doesn't like me. I stepped on her foot. I broke her claw.

I told her son she was weird and ugly.

I'm doomed. Doomed, I realized as I ran in panic through the long halls. Doomed—unless I can get out of here.

Mum and Dad.

Their faces flashed into my mind.

When they hear that my teacher is a monster, they'll be here in an hour.

No. No, they won't.

They won't believe me. They'll say Paul is at it again, blaming his teacher for his problems.

They'll say I have a bad attitude. They warned me to get along in this school.

But how can I get along with a monster that's going to slide me to the bottom of the food chain and then put my head on a cracker and eat me?

I have to make them believe me, I decided. They have to get me out of here.

I slowed to a walk. My heart pounded. My mouth suddenly felt so dry, I couldn't swallow.

I searched for a pay phone. Any kind of phone.

Why hadn't the other kids called for help? I wondered.

Molly, and Celeste, and Brad—and all the others—they knew this was serious. The girls had tried to warn me.

But why hadn't they called their parents? Why hadn't they tried to escape?

I turned a corner and made my way into the dorm area. No phones in the dorm rooms. No phones in the hall.

Finally, I spotted a pay phone hidden in a dark corner at the very end of the hall.

Gasping for breath, I lifted the receiver to my ear. I pressed zero.

"Hello? Hello—?" I shouted desperately. "Hello? Operator?"

"Operator? Hello?" I cried, my voice tiny and shrill.

A recorded voice rang in my ear: "Please hang up. Students may make outgoing calls only on holidays."

"Huh? Holidays?" I gasped. "I won't *live* till the next holiday!"

I'm going to be Mrs Maaargh's Thanksgiving turkey, I thought grimly.

I hung up. Then I picked up the phone again and tried dialling our phone number at home. But the same recorded voice told me to hang up.

I spun away, leaving the receiver dangling on its cord, the voice repeating its message over and over.

What am I going to do? I asked myself, struggling to keep my panic from tightening my throat, from making my knees tremble.

I've got to get out of this school. We *all* have to get away from here.

48

My heart pounding, I ran back to the canteen to find my friends. I spotted Molly, Celeste and Brad walking out, all three talking at once.

"There you are!" I cried breathlessly. "We have to leave! We have to get out of here!"

Celeste checked her watch. "We still have ten more minutes for lunch period," she said.

"How did it go with Mrs Maaargh?" Molly asked.

"She really *is* a monster!" I screamed. "She really *is* going to eat one of us!"

"Tell us something we don't know!" Celeste exclaimed. "We tried to warn you, Paul."

"But—but—" I sputtered. "Why are we standing here? Let's go! Let's get out of this place!"

Celeste sighed. "We can't. There's no way."

Brad shook his head. "We've tried. We've tried to escape a dozen times. There's no way to get out of this school!"

"We've already tried everything we could think of," Molly agreed. "*Everything*. As soon as we learnt about Mrs Maaargh, we tried to call out parents. But students—"

"Are only allowed to make calls on holidays. I know. I know," I moaned. "I tried to call too!"

"We all wrote letters home," Brad said. "But I think the school threw our letters out. Our parents didn't answer them."

"We tried to tell Mr Klane and some of the other teachers, but they didn't believe us,"

Celeste added. "They think we're making up wild stories just because Mrs Maaargh is strange looking."

"We have to do something!" I pleaded with them. "We can't just sit around here and do nothing! PLEASE!"

Molly sighed. She shook her fringe off her eyes. She looked so frightened. Tears formed in her eyes. "The only thing we can do is make sure we're not at the bottom of the food chain," she said softly.

"We've got to really practise for the talent show," Brad added. "You know, Mrs Maaargh is holding the auditions on Sunday afternoon."

"Sunday?" I gulped. "But I don't have a talent! I mean, I don't know what—"

"We're all doing reports for extra credit," Celeste told me. "You should start a report straight away, Paul. And make sure it's really good."

"A report?" I cried. "A report on *what*?"

"And a science project," Brad said. "We're all doing science projects for extra credit."

"But I've just arrived!" I protested. "I don't know what to do!"

Molly locked her dark eyes on mine. "If you don't have a talent, and you don't do extra projects. . ." Her voice trailed off.

We all knew what she was trying to say. She was saying that unless I acted fast, I was going to end up at the bottom of the food chain.

I stared from one to the other. How could I compete with them? They were super-students and they all had talents.

"This is crazy!" I cried. "I can't take this. No way! I'm going to see the headmistress! She's got to help us! She's got to believe us!"

"No, Paul! Wait!" I heard Molly's frightened cry.

"Wait—!" Celeste and Brad called.

But I didn't wait. I took off.

I can convince the headmistress that Mrs Maaargh is a monster, I told myself, hurtling through a startled group of students. I know I can convince her!

I'll drag her into Mrs Maaargh's classroom. I'll show her the food chain chart. And I'll show her the empty animal cages. And I'll make her listen to Celeste, Molly, Brad and everyone else in class.

They'll all tell her that Mrs Maaargh is a monster. She'll have to believe it when she hears it from *all* of us.

I flew down the hall. I hadn't met the head-mistress. But I knew where her office was. I had passed it when I entered the school this morning.

I checked my watch. The bell was about to ring for class. But I didn't care. This was more important.

51

I was saving a life. Probably mine.

I stopped at a door marked CARING ACADEMY HEADMISTRESS. The door was closed.

Struggling to catch my breath, I raised my hand and knocked on the glass.

After a few seconds, a voice called, "Come in."

She's in there! Thank goodness! I told myself.

I took a deep breath. Grabbed the knob and pushed open the door. "You have to help me!" I gasped.

"Help you? How?" The headmistress peered up from her desk.

And I opened my mouth in a shriek of horror.

"Wh-where's the headmistress?" I stammered. "I . . . uh . . . need to ask her a question."

Mrs Maaargh stood up behind the desk. "Paul, I am the headmistress," she said, her chins wagging beneath her lumpy yellow face. "Didn't anyone tell you that?"

"No!" I gasped. My hands were trembling. I shoved them into the pockets of my khakis.

"That's why I came here," the monster continued. "The school needed a new headmistress. But I love teaching. I can't stand being away from students. Teaching children is so . . . satisfying."

She stepped out from behind the desk. Her bare feet made wet, smacking sounds on the carpet. She began to circle me, her brown eyes studying me hungrily.

Her stomach growled. So loud, I jumped. It sounded like the gurgle of a bath emptying.

"I—I want to call my parents!" I blurted out.

She shook her head. Her cheeks wiggled like blubber. "It's not a holiday," she rasped.

"You can't do this!" I gasped. "It isn't . . . *human!*"

That made her smile grow wider. "I'm not human," she said. "I'm a monster."

"But—you can't eat kids!" I shrieked.

"I'm only eating one," she replied.

She slid her doughy hand under my chin. Her skin felt bumpy and damp. She brought her face close to mine. What was that smell on her breath? Mouse?

"You're a bit skinny," she whispered. "Have you been getting enough to eat?"

"I—I—" I stammered.

"Don't be so tense, Paul," she scolded. "You won't taste as good if you're tense."

"No!" I cried. "Let go!"

I tried to back away. But she tightened her hand on my throat. And narrowed her cow's eyes at me.

"Why do I have such a strong feeling that it's going to be you?" she demanded.

"No—!" I gasped. "No—it won't! It won't be me!"

She let her huge hand slide off my throat. Her smile returned. "Work hard, Paul," she said. "Work hard and do your best. Maybe you'll surprise me."

I spun away from her, my heart pounding,

my whole body shaking.

"Maybe you'll surprise me," she repeated. And then she added, "But I don't think so."

I staggered to the door. Tugged it open. Lurched into the hall.

The bell had rung. The long hallway stood silent and empty.

My wheezing breaths echoed off the tiled walls.

Where should I go? What should I do?

I only knew one thing. I had to prove her wrong. I wasn't going to be her human snack.

I can't go to class, I decided. I'll head back to my room. I'll stay in there and think. Try to come up with a plan.

Starting to jog, I turned a corner—and ran into Marv.

We both cried out in surprise.

"Hey," he muttered. He raised a small, brown paper bag. He reached a chubby hand in and pulled something out. "Here. For you," he said.

He held it out to me. Fudge. A large wedge of chocolate fudge. "You want it now?" He raised it to my face.

He's working with his mum, I realized.

He's trying to fatten me up!

"No way!" I screamed. I shoved him out of my way—and took off.

I had no idea what a big mistake I had just made!

After breakfast on Saturday morning, I followed Molly, Celeste and Brad to the music room. They planned to practise for the talent show auditions on Sunday afternoon.

"That Marv is such a pest," Brad complained.

I had just told them how Marv was trying to fatten me up for his mother. "Did Marv try to give you fudge too?" I asked Brad.

He shook his head as he clicked open his violin case. "No. I was practising my violin piece yesterday," Brad said. "Marv came into the music room. He wanted to try my violin."

Molly had her violin raised to her shoulder. She had started to tune it. "What did you do?" she asked Brad. "Did you let him try it?"

"No way that little creep is getting his paws on this!" Brad declared. "I kicked him out of here."

"He's just lonely," Celeste chimed in. "He

doesn't fit in here at this school. You should be nicer to him, Brad."

"No way!" Brad declared, tuning his instrument.

"Brad is right," Molly said. "Marv is a monster too. Don't forget it. He's very close to his mum. And now he's helping her frighten Paul."

"I'm not afraid of him," Brad muttered. "If he bothers me again, I'll punch out his lights."

Molly let out a sigh. She lowered her violin and turned to Brad. "I—I'm so scared, Brad. I can't believe you and I have to compete with each other. Why can't Mrs Maaargh let us *both* play violin in the talent show?"

"Don't worry about it," Brad replied. "I'm sure you'll find some other talent after I win the audition tomorrow!"

She stared at him in surprise.

Brad apologized. "Sorry. Just trying to keep it light. Wow. Everyone is so tense!"

"Of course we're tense!" Celeste exclaimed. "Someone is going to be *eaten*! Maybe someone in this room!"

I saw something move in the window of the music room door. I turned—and glimpsed Marv. Staring in at us with those round, black-marble eyes. Just staring at us so coldly, without blinking.

I shivered.

Marv moved away.

When I turned back to my friends, I found all three of them studying me. "What about *your* talent?" Celeste asked, peering at me over her glasses.

"Yes. What are you going to do, Paul?" Molly asked.

I shrugged. "I don't know. I stayed awake all last night thinking about it."

"And—?" Brad demanded. He scratched his spiky brown hair.

"Well . . . maybe I'll tell jokes," I said. "You know. Do a stand-up act."

"Bad idea," Celeste replied. "If your jokes don't make the audience laugh, Mrs Maaargh will definitely put you at the bottom of the chart."

"Yeah. It's too risky," Brad agreed.

"Then what am I going to do?" I cried shrilly. "I can't sing like you, Celeste. And I don't play a musical instrument. And—"

"I have an idea," Molly cut in. "It's a weird idea. But it's an idea."

We all turned to her. She rested her violin in her lap. "Balloon animals," she said.

I squinted at her. "Excuse me?"

"I just remembered my mum packed this box of balloons in my suitcase," Molly explained. "I bet you could teach yourself how to make some funny balloon animals. And you could tell jokes while you make them."

"That's a pretty cool idea," Brad said. "It could be funny."

"Yeah. Better than just standing up there telling jokes," Celeste added.

"Well. . ." I hesitated. "Okay. I'll try it. Thanks, Molly."

"You have to ask Mrs Maaargh," Brad said. "You have to get her permission."

"That's right. She has to approve every act," Celeste agreed.

"Go and get her permission," Molly said, tucking her violin in its case. "She's usually in the classroom on Saturday mornings. I'll get the box of balloons." She clicked the case shut, then hurried out of the music room.

I was in no big hurry to see Mrs Maaargh again. But I had no choice. I made my way down the long hall to the classroom.

I felt excited about the balloon act. I knew I could do some funny balloon animals. I knew I could do an act good enough to keep me from the bottom of the chart.

I took a deep breath and stepped into the darkened classroom.

"Mrs Maaargh?"

I glanced round. No sign of her. The lights were off. The blinds were pulled shut.

I clicked on the ceiling lights. "Anyone in here?"

As my eyes adjusted, I glimpsed the food

59

chain chart at the front of the room.

"Whooooa!" I let out a cry. My name had been moved down. Third from the bottom. Right above Molly and a boy named Peter Clarke.

Why had she moved me down so low? I wondered. Because I refused to eat Marv's fudge? Because I tried to use the phone?

Just because she doesn't like me?

"You're not going to get me," I said out loud. "I won't let you."

I turned to leave. But something at the back of the room caught my eye.

The bunny cage.

The door stood open wide.

Where was the bunny?

I took a few steps towards the cage—and stopped.

"Ohhhh." I let out a sick moan when I saw the thing on the floor.

At first, I thought it was a cotton ball.

But as I stared down at it, I knew what it was.

A fluffy white tail.

A fluffy white rabbit tail.

The bunny had gone.

Eaten.

Mrs Maaargh was working her way up the food chain.

Mrs Maaargh held the talent show auditions in the classroom, because the hall was being used by another group. "I know this is going to be enjoyable for all of us!" she gushed.

She wore a bright yellow dress that made her look bigger than the sun! Her hair was piled on her head like a heap of mud.

Mrs Maaargh was the only one in the room with a smile on her face. My classmates and I all sat stiffly, facing forwards.

No one talked. No one laughed. I heard a lot of throat clearing and saw a lot of nervous hands tapping on desks.

"I'm going to call you to come up and perform at random," the monster announced. "Remember, this is only an audition. It isn't the real show. But give it your best, people. Because I *will* be moving you up and down on the food chain today."

She looked straight at me when she

mentioned the food chain. And she licked her lips hungrily with that fat cow's tongue.

Celeste was called up first. She had a cassette with background music. She sang "My Favourite Things" from *The Sound of Music*, and did a beautiful job.

Mrs Maaargh moved her up to second on the food chain.

Peter Clarke, the boy on the bottom of the chart, did his act next. He made different musical notes by opening his mouth and slapping himself on the head. He played "The Star Spangled Banner" on his head. It sounded pretty good.

Mrs Maaargh moved him up four notches. That meant that Molly was at the bottom of the chart!

The night before, I'd asked Molly how she got to be so low on the food chain. It was after dinner, and I was practising making balloon animals as she rehearsed her violin number.

"Mrs Maaargh caught me trying to escape," Molly explained. "It was two days after school started. I was so frightened! I climbed out of a window and tried to run down the hill."

Molly sighed. "But Mrs Maaargh has video cameras all over the place. She caught me before I got halfway down. She dragged me back. The next day, she moved me down to the bottom."

Molly shook her head. "She's been on my back ever since," she murmured. "That's why I have to play my best at the audition. Otherwise. . ." Her voice trailed off.

"She's on my back too," I said. I held up my balloon animal. "Do you like this poodle?"

Molly stared at it. "Poodle? I thought it was a horse!"

Now I stared across the row at Molly. She was frantically tapping her fingers on the chair arm, waiting nervously for Mrs Maaargh to call on her.

But the teacher called the red-haired girl instead. She performed a modern dance. She did okay until she got cramp in her foot and had to stop.

Mrs Maaargh shook her head, but didn't move the girl up or down on the chart. The girl stayed in the middle of the food chain—and was really happy about it.

Mrs Maaargh called Molly next.

Molly played a short piece by Bach. She appeared nervous at first. In fact, when she started to play, her bow slipped right out of her hand.

But once she started, she was wonderful. Her fringe tilted and bobbed as she swayed with the music. When she'd finished, the whole class applauded.

She took a short bow and walked back to her seat. I could see that she was trembling. Sweat rolled down her forehead.

"Very good, Molly," Mrs Maaargh said. "We have one more violinist to hear from. Then I'll decide which of you will play at the talent show."

"But—but—" Molly stammered. "Aren't you going to move me up on the food chain?" She pointed to her name at the very bottom.

"No. I don't think so," Mrs Maaargh said.

"But why not?" Molly demanded.

"No reason," the teacher replied, crossing her blubbery arms in front of her yellow dress.

"But that's not fair!" Molly cried, her voice breaking.

"Of course it isn't fair," Mrs Maaargh snapped. "I'm a *monster*—remember?"

A few kids muttered low protests. But most people stared straight ahead in silence. We all knew that Molly had got a bad break. But I don't think anyone wanted to risk getting in trouble and taking her place at the bottom.

Mrs Maaargh called Brad next. "Let's see who is the better violin player," she said. She rubbed her doughy hands together. "I *love* a good competition. It really makes me work up an appetite!"

She laughed. She was the only one.

I shoved my hands into my pockets to keep

them from shaking. My mouth suddenly felt as dry as sand. I was really scared now. If Mrs Maaargh wasn't going to play fair, I was in big trouble.

She *hated* me!

I saw Molly still trembling at her desk. She covered her face with both hands.

Brad went to the music room to get his violin. We all waited in silence for him to return. Celeste flashed Molly a thumbs-up sign. I suppose she was trying to cheer up poor Molly. But Molly had her face covered and didn't see it.

Brad returned carrying his violin case and some sheet music. His hand was shaking when he set the music on the music stand. He kept clearing his throat and wiping sweat from his chin.

I could see that he was really terrified.

He opened the case with a quick snap of his wrists and flipped the top open.

He reached for the violin—and then stopped.

He shrank back. He let out a loud groan.

"No! Oh, nooooooo!" Brad wailed.

"Ohhhhh."

Kids sitting near Brad moaned too. Their faces twisted in disgust.

"It stinks!" someone cried.

"Oh, it smells so *bad*!" a girl wailed.

Brad staggered back from the case. He covered his nose and mouth with one hand. His eyes bulged in shock. He stared at the violin case as he backed away from it.

"Wow!" I let out a cry as the disgusting odour floated to the back of the room. It was sharp and sour. I held my breath, struggling to keep it out.

Several kids leapt up from their seats and moved to the window. The chubby boy from my row slid the window up and stuck his head outside.

"I can't *breathe*!"

"It's so awful!"

"Get it out! Get it out! Oh, I'm going to be sick!"

Cries and moans filled the room.

Brad backed up to the blackboard, both hands pressed over his face. I kept holding my breath, hoping the foul odour would go away.

Shaking her head, Mrs Maaargh stomped over to the violin case. She bent with a groan and lifted the violin from the case. Then she raised the instrument to her face.

She stuck her nose in the hole and took two or three long sniffs. "Smells like skunk," she announced. She set the violin back in its case. "I'll be right back."

She strode out of the door, her bare feet smacking the floor, her big yellow dress bobbing like a hot-air balloon.

All around the room, kids were choking and gagging. About a dozen kids had their heads out the windows, trying to breathe some fresh air.

Brad huddled at the wall, staring miserably at his violin, shaking his head.

Mrs Maaargh returned a few seconds later. She carried a small brown bottle in one hand. She stopped just inside the door and held up the bottle.

"It's skunk scent," she announced. "From the science lab upstairs. Pure skunk scent. I found it in the music room."

"But, who—?" Brad started. But he gagged from the odour. He held his nose and tried again. "Who would pour skunk scent into my violin?" he choked out.

Mrs Maaargh shrugged her broad shoulders. "Beats me," she said. Then she raised the brown bottle of skunk scent to her lips, tipped back her head, and took a long drink.

Kids groaned and cried out in disgust. More kids rushed for the window.

"Yep, it's skunk scent," Mrs Maaargh said, licking her lips.

Brad backed up till he was standing next to me at the back of the room. He kept swallowing hard, trying to keep from puking.

"My violin. . .?" he murmured. "I can't play now."

Mrs Maaargh's expression grew stern, angry. To my horror, she pointed an accusing finger— *at me*!

"*You* are responsible for this!" she growled.

"Huh? Me?" I gasped.

I started to stand up.

But then I realized Mrs Maaargh wasn't pointing at me. She was pointing at Brad.

"You are responsible for your own instrument," she told Brad.

"But—but—" Brad protested weakly.

"Molly will be our violinist," the teacher announced, sneering at Brad. "You will have to find another talent."

She marched over to the chart. Ripped Brad's name card from near the top of the chart. And stuck him at the very bottom of the food chain.

Molly let out a sob. "I'm so sorry, Brad," she murmured. "I didn't want to win this way."

Brad slumped on to the table holding the animal cages. Molly hurried back to him, shaking her head. She raised a hand to his shoulder. "You'll be okay," she whispered.

"You'll find something else."

Brad hung his head. He didn't reply.

The whole room was still going nuts from the smell. Kids were choking and gagging. Pleading with Mrs Maaargh to let them leave the room.

"We still have many more acts to audition," the monster insisted. "Get back to your seats, everyone."

She picked up the violin case and handed it to Brad. "Take this out of here. Then maybe the smell will go away."

Clamping his nose with one hand, Brad took the violin and, holding it out in front of him, hurried from the room.

"Paul will go next," Mrs Maaargh announced. "Seats, everyone! Seats!"

Oh, no. This isn't happening, I thought, shaking my head. How can I be so unlucky? The room still stinks. No one will be able to enjoy my act.

And then I saw the grin on Mrs Maaargh's face. And I realized she had deliberately picked me to go next.

I reached under my seat for the box of balloons. Not there. A sharp stab of panic shot through my chest. Then I remembered where I'd left them.

"The balloons are in my room," I told Mrs Maaargh. "Can I run and get them?"

She shrugged in reply.

I took that as a *yes*. I jumped from my seat and flew out of the room. I took deep breaths as I trotted to my room. Fresh air!

The skunk smell clung to my clothes. To my skin. I wondered if it would ever go away. I wanted to take a long, long shower. But, of course, I couldn't.

Time to do my act. I'd rehearsed most of the night. I'd worked up a pretty funny act.

Maybe, just maybe I can keep myself from the bottom, I told myself. *If* Mrs Maaargh plays fair.

I burst into my room. I saw Brad's sheet music scattered over his desk. Poor Brad, I thought. Mrs Maaargh didn't play fair with him.

Who poured the skunk scent into his violin? I wondered. Who would do such a horrible thing?

My eyes scanned the room. I spotted the box of balloons on my bed.

Weird, I thought. I could swear I'd left it on the top of my dressing-table.

I grabbed it in one hand and hurried out of the room. I walked quickly down the long hall to the classroom.

I grew more and more frightened with each step.

Will Mrs Maaargh like my balloon act? I

71

wondered. Will she think it's funny? Will she be fair? Will she give me a chance?

Taking a deep breath, I stepped into the classroom.

I took out a red balloon. "This is going to be an aardvark," I announced.

A few kids chuckled. Several kids still covered their noses and mouths. The skunk smell hung heavily over the room.

"Now it might *look* like a poodle!" I declared. "But take my word for it, it's an aardvark!"

I placed the red balloon to my lips and blew. And blew.

Nothing happened. The air fizzled through the balloon. But it didn't inflate.

"Ha-ha. Must be a hole in this one," I said. I threw the balloon aside. "All part of the act. To make it look harder."

A few kids chuckled.

I glanced at Mrs Maaargh. She had dropped into her wide desk chair. She leant over the desk with her big head propped in her hands and glared at me sternly.

"Okay! The first-ever balloon aardvark!" I

announced. I raised a long blue balloon to my lips and blew.

"Huh?"

It didn't inflate, either.

I tried again, raising it to my lips and huffing and puffing, blowing with all my strength. Slowly, the balloon filled up with air. I started to tie a knot in the end. But the balloon slowly deflated.

Some kids laughed. They must have thought it really was part of the act.

But I suddenly felt panic tighten my throat.

I threw the balloon aside and picked up another one. "Here comes the aardvark!" My voice cracked. My hands were shaking so badly, I could barely hold the balloon to my lips.

I took a deep breath, fighting back my panic.

I blew into the balloon.

The air fizzled right through it. The balloon made a loud *FFRRRRAAAP*.

A few kids laughed.

"No. Stop!" I cried shrilly. "This isn't right! Forget the aardvark. I'm going to go right to my hardest animal—a lobster!"

I picked up a long red balloon from the box and stretched it out between my hands. "A balloon lobster—with claws!" I announced.

Sweat poured down my forehead. The ceiling lights flashed in my eyes. The whole room appeared to tilt.

I raised the balloon to my mouth and blew.

Nothing. The air went right through it.

I pulled it out of my mouth and examined it. "What's going on? They can't *all* have holes in them!" I cried.

I spotted a tiny round hole at the tip of the balloon.

I pulled out a handful of balloons. I examined them one by one. A tiny pinprick hole in each balloon!

"They all have holes in them!" I cried. "Someone's poked a hole—"

Mrs Maaargh pulled herself up heavily to her feet. She sighed. "I think I've seen enough," she growled.

"But Mrs Maaargh—!" I pleaded. "I can't do my act. Someone's poked holes in my balloons!"

She *tsk-tsked*. Then she made her way over to the chart.

My name card made a loud *THWACK* as she pulled it off. She stuck the card below Brad's, at the bottom of the food chain.

Then she turned to me, licking her lips. "Be sure to eat your desserts, Paul," she said. "I want you nice and sweet."

"Marv did it," Molly said as we trudged back to our rooms.

The rest of the acts had gone well. A boy called Frank had ended up at the top of the chart, after reciting a long speech from *Hamlet*.

At the end of the auditions, I was still at the bottom, just below Brad. As I slumped down the long hall, I felt numb. Numb with fright.

I knew I'd stay at the bottom. I knew I was the one who would be eaten.

"Marv? What makes you say that?" Brad asked weakly.

"I saw him hanging around the music room this morning," Molly replied. "He put the skunk scent in your violin. I know he did."

"But why?" Brad demanded. "Because I wouldn't let him try my violin?"

Molly nodded. She turned to me. "I saw him in the hall outside your room," she said. "I bet he poked those holes in your balloons."

"Maybe," I replied in a choked whisper. I didn't feel like talking about it. I *couldn't* talk. I felt so angry and so terrified—at the same time.

"What are you going to do, Brad?" Molly asked. "Do you have another talent? You've got to think of something."

"I used to do card tricks when I was little," Brad replied, swallowing hard. "Maybe I'll work up a magic act."

We reached our room. I waved goodbye to Molly and slumped inside.

I stopped just inside the doorway—and cried out.

There on my dressing-table—resting on a white paper napkin—sat a large chunk of *fudge*!

So it *was* Marv! Marv had been in my room. Marv had punctured all the balloons.

He was still helping his mother. Still trying to fatten me up.

"*You can't do this to me!*" I shrieked. "*You can't!*"

I grabbed the fudge and heaved it out the open window. Then I threw myself on to the bed and buried my face in the pillow.

I met Molly and Celeste in the science lab after dinner. They were working together on a project for extra credit.

They had blue rubber balls attached to a structure of wires and poles. They were busily adding rubber balls, checking a chart in a textbook.

"What does it do?" I asked. My stomach growled. I hadn't been able to eat. I still felt shaky and upset.

"It doesn't do anything," Celeste explained. She curved a silvery wire around another wire. "It's a model of a galaxy."

I nodded. "Cool."

"You need a project, Paul," Molly warned. "Straight away."

"She's right," Celeste agreed. "You're at the bottom of the chart."

"You really don't have to remind me," I snarled.

"It's not *our* fault!" Molly cried. "Don't snap at *us*. We're only trying to help you."

"Sorry," I muttered. "I just don't see the point. . ." My sentence ended in a weak sigh.

"The point is, you've got to try harder," Molly urged. "You've got to do everything you can to impress Mrs Maaargh."

"I've already impressed her," I moaned, "as food! She thinks I'll make a terrific dinner."

Celeste turned away from the project. "You've got to raise yourself up from the bottom, Paul. You've got to try everything you can."

"Do a science project," Molly urged.

78

"Everyone is doing extra work. You have to try it too."

"I'm not like you lot," I wailed. "I don't belong in this school. I—I—"

"Don't lose it now," Celeste scolded, peering at me over her glasses. She brushed back her blonde curls. "You've got to keep it together, Paul. You don't have to finish at the bottom. You really don't."

"I have an idea for you," Molly said. She began flipping through pages in the textbook. "Here. Look at this."

I glanced down at a diagram. "What's that? A map of New Jersey?"

Celeste laughed. "At least you're getting your sense of humour back," she said.

"I always joke when I'm terrified," I murmured.

"It's a diagram of a molecule," Molly explained, jabbing her finger at the page. "It's the most complicated molecule ever discovered."

I rolled my eyes. "Thrills."

"Stop that attitude," Molly snapped. "Do you want help or not?"

I apologized again.

"You could build a model of this molecule," Molly continued. "It would really impress Mrs Maaargh."

I stared at the drawing. "Build it? How?"

Molly pulled open a drawer. "Look. There are

all these soft foam balls. And these sticks. You could build the molecule with this stuff. It would look great."

Celeste hurried to the corner of the lab and picked up a big cardboard box. "You can keep it in this. Bring your model in, unveil it, and surprise Mrs Maaargh."

I studied the diagram in the book. "So many parts to this thing," I groaned.

"You can do it," Celeste urged.

"You've got to try, Paul," Molly added.

They were right. I couldn't give up. I had to pull myself up from the bottom of the food chain.

So I set to work. I started pushing the soft foam balls on to the sticks. It was a bit like playing with the building sets I had when I was little. Except the molecule was very complex, very complicated.

We worked on our projects side by side. It would have been fun if I wasn't doing it out of total panic.

Molly and Celeste went back to their room at ten-thirty. But I kept working. I wanted to finish the molecule model as soon as possible. I was desperate to see if the project would help me.

A little before midnight, my eyes gave out. The sticks and balls were a blur. I couldn't read the diagram. The project was almost finished, but I was too tired to go on. I had to stop for the night.

I picked up the model and carefully slid it into the box. Then I closed the flaps on the box and tucked it away in the back of a cupboard.

Yawning, I shut off the lights of the science lab. Then I made my way down the long, silent hall towards the dorm rooms.

My shoes scraped loudly against the hard floor. The sound echoed down the hall. Everyone else had gone to bed, I supposed. Or they were in their rooms, studying hard.

I turned a corner—and gasped as a figure bounced out at me from a dark doorway.

"Marv!" I cried.

His black-marble eyes stared out at me from beneath his slicked-down hair. A cruel smile spread over his pale, round face.

"Paul," he whispered, "how did you like the fudge?"

"Leave me alone!" I screamed, my voice hoarse with terror.

I shoved him out of my way and ran to my room. I turned back at the door and saw Marv glaring at me. His face a scarlet red, his features twisted in anger.

I staggered into the room and shut the door behind me. I was breathing hard, blood pulsing at my temples.

Why is Marv doing this to me? I asked myself. I've never done anything to him. Why is he so eager to help his mother?

I turned and saw Brad sitting on the edge of his bed. He looked terrible. His hair had fallen down over his forehead. His eyes were red-rimmed and bloodshot.

He held up a pack of cards in both hands. "Paul, pick a card," he said. "Any card."

"I'm not really in the mood for card tricks," I replied, still struggling to catch my breath. I glanced at the wall clock. "It's after midnight, Brad. I—"

"You've *got* to help me!" he cried, jumping to his feet. "I've been working on these tricks for hours. Before that, I spent hours on the maths notebook I'm doing for extra credit. I've got to get these tricks to work."

A terrified sob escaped his throat. "I—I don't want to be eaten."

I shivered. "Neither do I," I murmured. "Marv has messed both of us up. He's ruined our chances."

"But we can come back!" Brad declared. "If we work hard, we won't finish at the bottom. We *can't!*"

He raised the pack of cards to me. I picked a card. I helped Brad with his card tricks for another two hours. Finally we had to stop. My eyes were burning. I was so tired, I couldn't tell a club from a diamond!

All the while, I kept glancing at the fresh box of balloons on my desk. I knew I should practise my balloon animals.

I'll practise tomorrow night, I promised myself. I'll study hard, and work on my model molecule, and make balloon animals—and maybe, maybe, maybe I will survive.

Yawning, I set my alarm clock, fell into bed, and slept a deep, dreamless sleep.

* * *

I woke up early the next morning, before the alarm went off. I pulled on khakis and a sweatshirt and hurried to my desk.

Still sleepy, I wrote a desperate letter to my parents. I told them my teacher was a monster. I begged them to come and rescue me—before it was too late.

Molly and Celeste had told me their letters weren't sent. But I had to try for myself. One last try.

I found a slot marked POST in the wall outside the front office.

I addressed my envelope carefully and put a stamp on it. Then I carried it to the postbox. No one was watching. So I slid it into the opening.

The office door was open. It was still early. No one seemed to be inside. I poked my head in—and gasped.

The postbox emptied into a large dustbin.

The girls were right. There was no way a letter was going to leave the school.

My heart pounding, I checked the door. No one out there.

I grabbed the phone off the front desk. I started to dial home.

But the taped message started up before I could finish dialling. "Please hang up. Students may make outgoing calls only on holidays."

Even the office phone was closed off!

No way to reach my parents.

I slumped upstairs to the science lab. I worked on my science project until it was time for breakfast.

I hope Mrs Maaargh likes it, I thought, shaking my head. I really hope she likes it.

I finished the model that night after dinner. It was an amazing tangle of sticks and little balls. I checked it and double-checked it against the diagram in the textbook. I had to make sure it was perfect.

Then I slid it carefully into its box and closed it up tight. I passed Molly and Celeste on my way back to my room and flashed them a thumbs-up.

Would my project impress Mrs Maaargh? Would it save my life?

There was only one way to find out.

The next morning, I carefully carried the box into the classroom. Mrs Maaargh was sorting papers at her desk. She had just arrived. It was fifteen minutes before class began.

She pretended she didn't see me. Kept her head down, shuffling the papers round her desk, grunting to herself.

I set the box down on the table beside her desk. "Mrs Maaargh?"

Finally, she glanced up at me. "You're early," she growled.

"I—I know," I stammered. I swallowed hard.

Had I ever been this nervous, this terrified in my life?

"What's in the box?" she motioned with her big head.

"A science project," I told her. "I've been working on it for days. It's a model. I did it for extra credit. I—hope you like it. I—"

"Just open the box and show it to me," she snarled.

I hesitated. "Uh . . . if you're in a bad mood, I could come back later. I mean—"

"Open the box!" she bellowed, her whole blobby face quivering.

I jumped. "Okay." I pulled up the flaps on the top of the box. "I worked very hard on it. It's a complicated model," I said. "Of a molecule. A very complicated molecule." I was so scared, I didn't even hear myself.

She tapped her fat, doughy fingers on her desk.

I carefully slid the model out from the box and set it on her desk. "Do you like it, Mrs Maaargh?"

She stared at it. Her watery eyes bulged. And her mouth dropped open in a startled gasp.

"*Is . . . this . . . a joke?*" she rasped.

Huh?

I turned and stared at the model. "Oh, no!" I shrieked.

Someone had changed it. Someone had moved everything around.

It wasn't my molecule. It wasn't *any* molecule.

The sticks and balls—they spelled out two words: YOU UGLY.

With a furious growl, Mrs Maaargh grabbed the project and crushed it between her hands. Sticks cracked and balls bounced off the desk and over the floor.

"I—I didn't—" I tried to explain.

"*It . . . isn't . . . even . . . good . . . grammar!*" she bellowed.

She hoisted herself up with a loud grunt. Stomped over to the food chain chart.

"Mrs Maaargh—please!" I begged.

She ripped my name off the bottom of the chart and pressed it on to the floor. "You're not even on the chart!" she raged.

"But—but, please—"

"You're so low, Paul, you're on the floor!" the monster cried. "You're not even on the chart!"

I opened my mouth to protest. But only a terrified squeak escaped.

As I stood there shaking, the monster brought her face down close to mine. "You have a *new* name now," she rasped, her hot, wet breath spraying my ear. "You're not Paul any more. Your new name is *Lunch Meat!*"

My legs were trembling. My whole body was trembling. But somehow I managed to spin away from her. And stagger weakly out of the room.

I lurched down the hall, my head spinning. Students were beginning to pour out of their rooms. I didn't want to see anyone. I didn't want to talk to anyone.

I had to get back to my room and *think*. I had to work out what to do next.

What *could* I do?

I stumbled through a group of girls. Turned a corner. And saw Marv.

He flashed me another cruel smile. A knowing smile.

He was letting me know that he had struck again.

He started to say something. But I hurried past him, twisting through the clusters of kids heading to class.

"Paul—what's wrong?"

I turned and saw Molly running after me, her expression worried, upset. "What's happened, Paul?"

I didn't want to talk to her. I couldn't face her now. She had tried to help me. But it was all a waste of time.

A complete waste.

She and Celeste stared at me as I took off. I ran to my room and slammed the door. I threw myself on the bed. Then jumped up. Paced the room. Threw myself into a chair. Jumped up again.

I didn't know what to do with myself.

"Whyyyyyyy meeeeeeee?" I howled. I slammed the wall with my fist.

And suddenly I knew what I had to do.

Escape.

I had no other way to survive.

My name was Lunch Meat. Mrs Maaargh said so herself. I was too low to be on the food chain.

Escape. It was my only chance.

I knew Molly and the others had tried it. I remembered that Molly had said it was impossible.

But maybe I'd get lucky. Maybe I could sneak out of the building. Make my way down the steep hill. Find someone, someone who would listen to me. Someone who would believe me. Someone to come back to the school and rescue everyone else in the class.

I rubbed my fist. It throbbed from slamming against the wall. But I hardly noticed it.

I knew what I had to do. Escape. I had to try.

After all, I had nothing to lose.

* * *

I didn't go to class. I called the nurse's office and said I was sick.

I waited until all the other kids were in their classrooms. Then I went exploring.

I crept from doorway to doorway, keeping out of sight of teachers and anyone else walking in the hall. I made my way up and down the halls until I found what I was searching for.

A small doorway next to the kitchen pantry at the back of the school. The door wasn't used by students or teachers. It was used by kitchen workers to bring in supplies.

If I pulled it open, would it set off an alarm?

I had to try it. I took a deep breath. Turned the knob. And pulled.

The heavy door swung open.

I didn't hear a bell or a siren.

No alarm.

Excellent!

I peered out. Dark clouds hung heavily in the sky. The air felt cool and moist. I realized it had been days since I'd breathed fresh air.

I lowered my gaze down the hill. I couldn't see a fence or any alarm system out there. Nothing to keep me from running down the hill, from getting away.

Maybe there were video cameras watching the door and the back of the building. But I couldn't see any. And if I ran fast enough, maybe I'd escape.

And once I got down the hill, if I kept walking, eventually I was bound to find a house or a town—or somebody!

I gasped as I heard footsteps approaching.

I pulled my head in and closed the door. I spun round as two white-uniformed women approached.

"What are *you* doing back here?" one of them demanded, straightening her hairnet.

"Uh . . . I got a bit confused," I replied. "I was looking for the canteen."

"It's that way," she replied, pointing. "But you're too late for breakfast and too early for lunch."

"Oh. Sorry," I said. I took off down the hall. I could feel their eyes on my back as I hurried away.

But I didn't care about them.

I was going to escape. I had found the way out. And I was going to take it.

The next morning, a heavy rain spattered the room window. Thunder roared.

I didn't care. I thought the rain would make it harder for them to chase after me.

I went to breakfast with Brad. I tried to act normally. I tried to act as if nothing unusual was about to happen.

I waved across the canteen to Molly and Celeste. I talked to Brad about my balloon animals. I pretended I was worried about the talent show.

I wanted to tell him my plan. I wanted to tell Molly and Celeste too. I wanted to ask them to escape with me.

But I didn't want to risk anyone overhearing.

What if Marv was lurking around?

And I figured it would be easier for one person to slip out than two or more.

I'll come back with help, I told myself. I'll rescue them all.

I stood up in the middle of breakfast. I made my way towards the toilets at the back. But outside the canteen, I turned.

And crept to the back door I had found.

I didn't wait. I didn't hesitate.

I tugged open the door—and hurtled out into the pouring rain.

"Whooooa!"

I cried out as waves of rain battered me. I ducked my head and ran through *walls* of falling water.

My shoes skidded over a narrow concrete driveway. Puddles rose up over my ankles. I splashed up tall, cold waves as I ran.

On to tall grass now. The hill sloped down in front of me.

But the rain came down so hard, it formed a solid curtain of water. I couldn't see the bottom of the hill. Or the deep woods that stretched beyond it.

I could barely see a metre in front of me!

My feet kept skidding out from under me. I had to slow my pace. My drenched clothing clung to my skin. I tried to shield my eyes with one hand as water rolled down my forehead.

Lightning crackled low overhead. Thunder boomed all around me.

94

I ducked my head and ran.

Let it rain! I told myself. Let it pour! I'm getting away. I'm doing it. I'm escaping from that horrible place.

I couldn't stop myself. I threw back my head. And opened my mouth in a joyful laugh.

I'm doing it! I'm doing it!

"Hey—!" I cried out as my foot caught in some kind of rut.

I threw up my hands. Struggled to keep my balance. But my feet slid out from under me.

I landed hard on my back in the wet grass. My body sank into the soft ground.

Rain beat against me, wave after wave of freezing water.

I scrambled to my knees. My ankle ached, but I could move it. It was okay.

I started to my feet—and heard a cry behind me.

The roar of the rain was so loud, I couldn't make out the words.

I stood up shakily, brushing a clump of mud off my sweatshirt.

And then I heard the cry again. Closer.

"Paul! Paul! Stop!"

I'd been caught.

Through the thundering, grey sheets of rain, I could see a figure running towards me over the grass. I saw arms waving wildly.

And again, the cry: "Paul—stop! Stop!"

A flash of lightning made the sky brighter than day. And in that flash, I saw Molly's frantic face, her wild eyes, her hands waving above her head.

I had a strong urge to turn away and keep running.

But she was beside me before I could move, gasping for breath, bending over, pressing her hands against the soaked knees of her jeans.

"Paul—" she gasped. Her black hair was drenched, matted to her forehead. "Where—?"

"We can escape!" I cried, shouting over the roar of rain. "There's no fence, Molly! Nothing to stop us!"

I motioned towards the bottom of the hill. But

she grabbed my arm and pulled me back towards the school.

"Invisible!" she shouted.

"Huh?" I squinted at her through the rain.

She cupped her hands around her mouth. "The fence—it's invisible! Electric! Like for dogs. To keep dogs in the yard."

I nodded. I understood.

"You'll get a shock," Molly shouted. "I know! I've tried. . ." The rest of her words were drowned out by a crash of thunder.

"But Molly—I've got to try," I cried. "I can't stay there."

"You have to come back!" Molly insisted. She pulled my arm harder. Almost pulled me over.

"Let go!" I shouted. "I don't want to—"

"You don't understand! You have to come back!" she repeated. "Your parents are here!"

My heart actually skipped a beat.

My mouth dropped open. "Really?" I gasped.

She nodded and tugged me again.

My parents? They were here? How did they know? How did they know I needed to be saved? That we all needed to be saved?

Molly and I ran side by side, leaping over deep lakes of rainwater, slipping and skidding over the tall grass, up the hill.

The ugly, dark school rose up in front of us. Lightning crackled between its black towers.

We burst in through the back door, trailing rivers of water behind us. "Where are they?" I gasped. "Where?"

Molly pointed. "I saw them standing out the front. Near the classrooms." She pushed me. "Quick. Go and change."

I shivered. "There isn't time. I—"

"Go and change," Molly insisted. "If they see

98

you like that, they won't listen to a word you say."

She was right.

I hurried to my room, sliding and slipping, shaking off water as I ran. I threw my soaked clothes in a heap on the floor and pulled on dry khakis, a black shirt and a dry pair of trainers.

My heart thudded in my chest. I couldn't wait to see them. I felt so happy. So relieved. So *safe*.

I tore through the halls. I ran full speed, my trainers thundering over the hard floor. My chest felt about to burst.

I spotted them outside a classroom. "Mum! Dad!" I shouted breathlessly, waving wildly with both hands.

They turned and waved back.

"I'm so glad to see you!" I choked out. "How did you know—"

"Paul—slow down. Slow down!" Dad exclaimed.

Mum frowned at me. "Mrs Maaargh tells us you're having problems. Paul, we're very disappointed."

"She's a *monster*!" I screamed. "A *monster*!"

Mrs Maaargh poked her head out of the classroom door. "See what I mean?" she said to my parents. "See what I mean?"

"But—but—" I sputtered.

"Come to the teachers' lounge," Mrs Maaargh said pleasantly. "We can have a nice, private chat." She flashed me a sick smile.

"Mum—listen to me!" I pleaded.

Mrs Maaargh's bare feet smacked the floor as she led the way across the hall to the teachers' lounge.

"Paul, you're drenched!" Mum exclaimed. "Why is your hair soaking wet?"

"Well . . . I tried—"

"He tried to run away this morning," Mrs Maaargh cut in.

Both of my parents let out startled gasps.

"Yes. It's true," Mrs Maaargh told them, clicking on the light. "I told you, he seems very troubled."

Both of my parents glared at me sternly.

"We'll have a cup of tea and a snack," Mrs Maaargh said sweetly. She leant towards me and licked her lips. "A snack—always a good way to start the day."

Mum and Dad took seats around a wooden table and forced me to join them. "Paul has trouble adjusting to new schools," Mum told Mrs Maaargh.

"I felt I had to call you," Mrs Maaargh said, pouring out cups of tea.

"Huh?" I cried, jumping up from my seat. "You called *them*?"

"I thought you might want to take Paul home," Mrs Maaargh said, handing a steaming cup to each of them. "Since he seems to be unhappy here."

"Yes!" I cried, shooting my fists in the air. "Yes! Take me home! Take me home!"

"Of *course* we don't want to take him home," Dad said, frowning at me. "We want Paul to stick it out. He has to learn to adjust."

"We hope you will give him a second chance," Mum said to Mrs Maaargh. "Please don't send him home."

The teacher nodded, her chins folding over the front of her dress. "No need to worry," she said sweetly. "After our little chat today, I'm sure that all of Paul's problems will be over."

I shuddered. And jumped to my feet. "You *have* to take me home!" I shrieked.

"Paul, sit down—right now!" Dad snapped.

"But she's a *monster*!" I cried, pointing at Mrs

101

Maaargh. "I'm telling the truth!"

"That's enough!" Mum shouted. "Why are you acting like such a baby?"

"You've got to believe me!" I begged. "She's a monster. Look at her feet. Look at them!"

Dad shook his head. Mum blushed. "I'm so sorry," Dad told Mrs Maaargh. "I apologize for Paul. I don't know what to say."

"Please." Mrs Maaargh held up a doughy hand. "No harm done. I know the kids make fun of my feet. They're very swollen."

She stepped back. Her feet made wet, smacking sounds. She gazed down at them, shaking her enormous head sadly.

"It's my glands," the monster murmured. "The doctors say they've never seen such a bad case. I'm taking medicine for it."

Mum *tsk-tsked*.

Mrs Maaargh picked a piece of lint off one of her curled, black claws.

"I can't squeeze my swollen feet into shoes," Mrs Maaargh continued sadly. "I'm very embarrassed about it."

"You shouldn't be embarrassed," Mum told her. She turned to me. "Paul should be embarrassed for being so rude."

"You don't understand—" I started.

But Dad motioned for me to sit down and shut up.

"I'm worried about Paul," Mrs Maaargh said,

sipping her tea noisily. Her fat tongue splashed around in the cup. "It's very dangerous to try to run away."

"He won't run away again," Dad said. "I promise you that."

"But—but—" I struggled desperately to tell them the truth. But Mum and Dad kept hushing me.

"The woods are so dangerous," Mrs Maaargh continued. "If he tries to run away again, he could be lost. He could be lost for ever."

Oh, wow!

Suddenly, it all became clear to me. Suddenly, I realized the real reason Mrs Maaargh had called my parents to school.

She was paving the way for me to disappear!

She was going to eat me for dinner. And then she was going to tell my parents I'd run away from school and disappeared in the woods.

And then she would say with tears in her big, cowlike eyes, *I warned you this could happen. I warned Paul not to run away.*

My parents chatted a little while longer with Mrs Maaargh. Then the teacher slurped the rest of her tea and stood up from the table.

"It's been a pleasure meeting you," Mrs Maaargh rattled with that phony sweet smile. "I really must start class."

"Thank you for talking to us," Dad replied, shaking her fat hand.

"We know that Paul will try harder from now on," Mum said, her eyes trained on me.

"Paul, I hope you got the message here today," Mrs Maaargh said, grinning an ugly grin at me. "You know what?" She leant close to me. "I'm going to let *you* perform first at the talent show tomorrow."

"You're having a talent show?" Mum exclaimed. "How wonderful! I wish we could stay for it. What a wonderful school!"

Mrs Maaargh said goodbye again and lumbered out of the door.

As soon as she had gone, I jumped up and turned to my parents. "How could you believe her?" I shrieked. "How could you believe her and not me?"

"She seems like a very nice person," Mum replied.

"Paul, what exactly is your problem?" Dad demanded.

"She's a *monster*!" I shrieked. "A *monster*!"

Dad scratched his head. "She *is* a little strange looking," he admitted. He frowned at me. "But we brought you up never to judge people by their looks—remember?"

"Beauty is only skin-deep," Mum added.

They walked to the door.

I grabbed Dad's sleeve. "But she's going to *eat* me!" I screamed. "Don't you understand? She's going to eat me alive!"

Mum and Dad both laughed. "Tell her to use plenty of ketchup," Dad said.

"Tell her to save the wishbone for me," Mum joked.

Jokes?

We were at the front door. They hugged me. They told me to stop making up stupid stories. They told me to be a good student. They hugged me again.

And then they were gone.

They were my last chance. And they were gone.

I stood there, staring at the front door until it became a dark blur.

What do I do now? I asked myself. What do you do after your last chance has gone?

Is there any way I can save myself?

A hard tap on my shoulder made me scream.

I jumped and spun round, my heart pounding.

"Marv!"

His tiny eyes flashed in his round, molelike face. He grinned and held up a red and yellow packet. "Would you like some biscuits?" he asked.

I had one last chance.

I knew my situation was desperate. My parents had already been warned that I might disappear. Mrs Maaargh was calling me "Lunch Meat" in front of everyone.

But there is always one last chance—right?

I stayed up all night practising my act for the talent show. First I made Molly and Celeste watch. Then I returned to the room and forced Brad to watch me for hours.

My balloon animals were amazing. They all agreed. They said they'd never seen *anyone* do a balloon armadillo before. And my balloon elephant, which took eight balloons to build, was incredible!

And I had very funny jokes to go with each animal.

I stayed up rehearsing, hour after hour. I didn't get sleepy. I was too nervous, too frightened.

But the more I practised, the better I felt. The balloon act could save me, I decided. If I don't mess it up, if I perform well on that stage, I just might be able to pull myself up the food chain.

The talent show was scheduled for right after breakfast. I sat in the canteen and stared down at my scrambled eggs and bacon.

My stomach was a rock. I felt as if all the muscles in my body were tied in knots. I knew I needed energy to perform my best. But I just couldn't eat.

"Paul?" A woman's voice made me look up from my eggs. The office secretary stood behind my table. "There's a note for you," she said. "In the front office."

I followed her out of the canteen. I could see everyone staring at me. She led the way to the office near the front of the school.

"There," the secretary said, pointing. She hurried to answer a ringing phone.

I picked up the folded note from the counter. Unfolded it and read it.

I read the signature at the bottom first. The note was from Mrs Maaargh. She had surprisingly dainty handwriting:

It's show time! You will be first this morning. Please meet me in the middle of the main hall's stage. Come when you receive

this note, and we will get everything ready.
Mrs Maaargh

I swallowed hard. My mouth suddenly felt dry as sand. I bent down and took a long drink from the water fountain outside the office.

Then I hurried to my room to get my box of balloons.

This is it! I told myself. This is my last chance to save myself.

I passed the canteen. Kids were still eating. I still didn't feel hungry. I grabbed the balloons and made my way to the hall.

I pulled open a door and stepped inside. To my surprise, the big hall was completely dark. The only light came from a yellow spotlight that threw a circle of light on to the centre of the stage.

I bet that's where Mrs Maaargh wants me to wait, I decided.

My eyes searched the seats and then the stage. Where was she?

My legs felt weak and trembly as I climbed on to the stage. I gripped the box of balloons tightly, as if it were a life-jacket.

"Mrs Maaargh?" I called, squinting into the shadows backstage. "Mrs Maaargh? I'm here!" My voice echoed over the rows and rows of empty seats.

"Shouldn't someone turn on the hall lights?" I called.

No reply. No one around.

I stepped into the circle of light from the spotlight. I waited for my eyes to adjust to the brightness.

"Hello?" I called. "Anyone here? Hello?"

I held up the box of balloons. I recited the opening line of my act, just to see how it felt. "Hello, everyone, I'm your friendly, local balloonatic!"

I imagined everyone in the seats in front of me laughing loudly at that. I pictured Mrs Maaargh grinning, thinking to herself, *Paul isn't so bad after all. Maybe I'll give the kid a break.*

"Mrs Maaargh?" I called. "Are you here?"

As I stood under the hot light, sweat poured down my forehead. I felt hot, then cold. My hands were wet and ice cold.

My last chance, I thought. Let's get going!

At the back of the hall, a door opened. Light poured over the back aisle. A girl poked her head into the light.

Molly!

I squinted past the rows of seats. Holding on to the door, she stared up at the stage.

"Paul?" she called. "What are you doing up there?"

"I'm waiting for Mrs Maaargh," I told her,

shouting so she could hear. "I'm going to perform first."

Her mouth dropped open. "Didn't you hear?
They announced it at breakfast."

"Announced what?" I shouted.

"The talent show has been cancelled!"

Molly vanished. The door closed, shutting out the light.

I stood there in shock for a long moment, staring out into the darkness.

Cancelled? Cancelled?

With a long sigh, I started to step out of the spotlight.

And a hand grabbed me roughly round the back of the neck.

I gasped.

The hand tightened round me.

I jerked round—and saw Mrs Maaargh. She held me by the neck. Lowering her huge head close to mine, she opened her mouth in a wide grin.

"*Good morning, BREAKFAST!*" she growled.

"N-no!" I stammered. I squirmed. I twisted.

She was too strong. I couldn't break free.

I let out a sharp cry as we started to sink.

What was happening? Was the whole school

sinking into the ground?

No. I saw to my horror that we were standing on a trapdoor hidden in the stage floor. The trapdoor was lowering, sliding down rapidly.

"Where are we going?" I shrieked. "What are you doing?"

She licked her lips hungrily in reply.

I shot up my arms. Tried to push her away.

Her hand wrapped around my neck. She held on tightly.

The trapdoor slid down beneath the stage. I saw only darkness now. My legs trembled. I started to fall to my knees. But the monster held me up with her one-handed grip on my neck.

"You—you don't really want to do this!" I choked out.

"Sure I do," she rumbled.

The trapdoor carried us down . . . down. . .

"But—you're going to feel so sorry," I told her.

"No, I won't," she replied, chuckling. "I'm a *monster*, remember?"

"But it isn't *right*!" I squealed. "You know it isn't right!"

"I don't know right from wrong," she growled. "I only know I'm hungry."

"But—but—" I sputtered. "You'll get caught! They'll find out and catch you! They'll kill you!"

"That's why I'm careful," she rasped, her hot,

sour breath blowing over my face. "That's why I only eat one a year!"

The trapdoor bumped to a stop. I squinted into total blackness.

Mrs Maaargh pulled me by the neck, pulled me roughly off the trapdoor. As I stumbled away, I heard it begin to hum back up to the stage.

I'm trapped down here, I realized. But where are we?

Grunting softly to herself, Mrs Maaargh dragged me down a long, dark tunnel. We turned a corner and made our way through another tunnel.

It opened into a wide, low basement room. Dust-covered pipes ran along the walls and ceiling. I heard water dripping somewhere. Machines humming. A rumbling noise up ahead.

The monster reached up with her free hand and clicked on a bare light bulb. It cast pale light over the grey, dusty basement room.

"Where are we?" I gasped. "What are we doing down here?"

She dragged me to the wall. Reached down and flung open a big metal door.

I heard a roar. Flames jumped behind the door, crackling and spitting loudly.

"The furnace!" I cried.

Mrs Maaargh brought her face close to mine.

"I'm not an animal!" she growled. "I don't eat my meat raw! I cook it first!"

Holding me tightly, she opened her mouth wide. Her gums began to swell. Four rows of crooked teeth curled out from them. Thick gobs of white saliva rolled down the ugly teeth.

She began grunting loudly. Her chest heaved up and down. Her fat tongue rolled over the rows of teeth.

She lifted me off the floor with both hands.

"No, please—!" I begged. I stared at the jumping flames inside the roaring furnace. "Wait—! Please!"

She snapped her jaws hungrily.

Then she raised me high in front of her—and heaved me into the flames.

"Noooooooo!" I let out a long scream.

I shot out my arms and legs.

And grabbed the furnace door.

With a hard twist, I swung myself away from the flames.

And dropped to my feet beside the open furnace door.

The monster tilted back her head in an angry roar. She dived for me—but I stumbled out of her grasp.

I picked up a heavy metal shovel. A shovel used to stoke the furnace. With a groan, I raised it over my head—and flung it with all my might at the monster.

The shovel blade caught her in the stomach.

The monster uttered a startled cry and doubled over.

Had I hurt her?

I didn't wait to find out.

I took off, running down the long tunnel, my

arms stretched out in front of me as if grabbing for safety.

I ran full speed, gasping for breath, not turning back, not listening, not seeing anything but the darkness of the tunnel ahead.

I turned and ran down the next tunnel.

Up ahead, I heard a low hum. I saw shoes. Then jeans legs.

The trapdoor! Someone was on it! Someone had taken it down to the basement!

I stumbled to a stop. "Molly—?" I gasped. "What are you—how did you—?" I was breathing too hard to talk.

"Paul, I'm sorry," Molly cried. "Hurry. Get on."

"Sorry?" I whispered. "What do you mean?"

"Sorry I did this to you!" she said with a sob. "But I was so scared, Paul. So scared. I knew Mrs Maaargh was going to eat me. She hated me, because I tried to escape. I was going to be her victim, Paul. I was so scared. Then you arrived."

"But—but—I don't understand!" I exclaimed.

"I knew it was wrong," Molly continued, shaking all over. "But I did all those horrible things. I ruined Brad's violin so I could be the violinist. Then I poked the holes in your balloons. And changed your model. I was terrified. I didn't want to be eaten."

"But yesterday," I said, "you came after me in

the rain. Why—?"

"I couldn't let you escape," Molly said, sobbing again. "If you escaped, I knew I'd be eaten! So I made you come back. I was so selfish, so cruel. But I couldn't help myself. I was just so *scared*!"

I stared at her, my mouth hanging open. It wasn't Marv. It was Molly all along.

"But I couldn't go through with it," Molly cried. "I couldn't live with myself. So I came down to rescue you."

The trapdoor lift hummed and bumped into motion. It began to rise.

"Hurry, Paul." Molly reached out for me. "Jump on. We can get away."

"Okay!" I cried. The lift was already up to my waist, climbing fast.

I made a leap for it.

But something held me back.

"*Where are you going, BREAKFAST?*" Mrs Maaargh growled. She had her fat arms wrapped around my legs.

I reached both hands for Molly. "Wait! Wait!" I pleaded.

But the lift carried Molly away.

"Too bad," the monster snarled. A cruel smile spread over her face. "Bye, bye, lift. Bye, bye, Paul!"

"No—!" I screamed.

I twisted free of her grasp.

I can outrun her, I told myself. She's big and she's slow. I can outrun her.

But where can I run?

She rose up, preparing to tackle me again.

I shoved past her and took off.

I ran blindly down the tunnel. Was there a door? Some steps? A good hiding-place?

I hurtled through the darkness.

Turned a corner. Down another hall. Past a cluttered supply room. Into another tunnel.

"Nooo!" I let out a startled shriek as I ran right into Marv.

"Please!" I gasped. "Please—don't tell her where I am. Let me get away!"

His little eyes widened in surprise. He stepped back. "You're my friend," he murmured.

I had started to run past him. But I stopped and turned back. "Excuse me?"

"You're my friend," he repeated. "You sat with me in the canteen. You were the only one. You were the only one to talk to me. The only one to be nice to me."

I swallowed hard. "You mean—"

"That's why I brought you sweets," he said. "Because you were my friend."

"You're not helping your mother?" I gasped.

He shook his head. "I'll help *you!*" he declared.

I heard rumbling footsteps behind us in the tunnel, growing louder. Mrs Maaargh was tracking me down.

"Help me? How?" I demanded. "Can you get

me out of here?"

He shook his head again. "No way out," he murmured.

"Then how can you help me?" I shrieked.

The monster's heavy footsteps plodded closer.

"Make her laugh," Marv said.

I squinted at him. "Say that again?"

"Make her laugh, Paul. She almost never laughs. But when she does laugh, she goes into hibernation. She will fall asleep and sleep for six months."

"But how?" I cried, frantically grabbing the front of his baggy shirt. "How can I make her laugh?"

He didn't reply. His eyes bulged. He tore free of my grasp and backed into the shadows.

I turned and saw why he'd shrunk back.

Mrs Maaargh stood in front of me, breathing hard, blocking the tunnel. Arms out at her sides, she lowered her head and snarled at me, preparing to attack one more time.

"Nowhere to run now, Breakfast," she rattled. She licked her lips hungrily. And opened her mouth, once again revealing the four rows of teeth.

I stared at her in horror. How can I make her laugh? I asked myself. What can I say? What can I do?

My brain whirred so hard, I felt as if my head might explode.

Should I tell her jokes?

No. She never laughed at my jokes. Besides, I was too terrified to remember any jokes.

If only I had my balloons, I thought. My balloon armadillo would make her laugh.

What else could I do?

Dance? Sing?

No. No way. She'd gobble me up before I had a chance to finish.

What could make her laugh? *What?*

Growling softly, she lowered her head and prepared to attack.

Suddenly, I had an idea.

The monster lumbered forwards, her big feet smacking the concrete floor.

I dropped to my knees.

"What are you doing?" she bellowed.

I bent down. Reached out my hand.

Could I do it? Could I *touch* those disgusting, wet, pillow feet?

She tapped one of the feet on the floor impatiently. *SMACK. SMACK.* The thick claws clicked against the floor.

I raised my fingers over the foot.

My stomach churned. I felt sick!

I can't touch it, I thought. It's too horrible!

"Get up!" she snarled.

I brought my hand down over the foot. I had no choice. I had to do it.

I ran my fingers lightly over the top of the bulging foot.

So soft. So mushy. So moist.

I began to tickle.

122

Bent down on the floor, I couldn't see the monster's face. But I heard her gasp.

I tickled the foot some more. Moved my fingertips up and down the mushy, soft skin.

Yuck, I thought. This is sick. This is so sick.

I can't believe I'm *touching* these things.

But, to my amazement, Mrs Maaargh began to laugh.

I tickled harder.

Her laughter rang out through the long basement tunnels. Harsh, hoarse laughter that sounded more like a dog barking than laughter.

I ran my fingers up and down the disgusting foot.

She laughed and laughed. Hiccuped and laughed.

And then she slumped heavily to the floor. Plopped down into a sitting position. Laughing with her head thrown back.

Laughing . . . until her head fell back.

Her whole body tumbled back . . . until she was lying flat on the floor.

I climbed quickly to my feet, my stomach churning. My fingers tingled. My whole body itched and tingled.

Her chest and stomach heaved up and down. She was stretched out on the floor, breathing steadily, heavily. Eyes closed, mouth slightly open.

"She's asleep," Marv said quietly, stepping out of the shadows.

I stared down at her. I still felt too sick to speak. I could feel the wet touch of her foot on my fingers.

"She'll sleep like that for months," Marv said. "Maybe a year."

I forced myself to turn away from her. "You—you saved my life," I gasped.

A smile spread over Marv's round face. He tugged at one side of his slicked-down hair. "I suppose so."

I put my arm around his shoulders. "You saved my life!" I cried joyfully. "I can't believe it! You saved my life!"

We started to walk towards the trapdoor lift. Marv stopped. He turned to me. "There's just one problem, Paul."

"What's that?" I asked.

His little black eyes glowed. "All that excitement has made me really hungry!" he said.

I gasped and pulled away from him. "You're kidding," I cried. "You're kidding—right?

"Right?"